MW00618970

The Dog Who Found a Body

Body

(A Tail Waggin' Mystery)
By Cynthia Hickey

Copyright © **2021 Cynthia Hickey**
Published by: Winged Publications

This book is a work of fiction. Names, characters, places, and incidents are the product of the author's imagination and are used fictitiously. Any resemblance to actual events, locales, or persons, living or dead, is coincidental.

No part of this book may be copied or distributed without the author's consent.

All rights reserved.

ISBN: 978-1-952661-58-7

To all the cozy mystery readers who love quirky characters, rowdy pets, a hero with a bit of a stubborn streak, and a hero that lets her be who she is.

.

Chapter One
"Sheba!" Oh, that dog.

I watched in dismay as the mastiff puppy I'd adopted ran across the park and leaped into the pond splashing nearby hikers who shrieked and jumped back. When I'd found her as a stray, I thought her full grown. The vet said six months old. How big would she get? And would she ever listen to my commands?

Taking off at a run, I stopped at the water's edge. "Come back here, you crazy mutt." Misbehaving or not, I couldn't help but laugh at her antics, which only served to encourage her. "Fine. I'm continuing the hike without you." Clutching her leash, which I vowed never to remove again, I set off down the path, casting an eye over my shoulder.

Not to be left behind, Sheba bounded after me, spraying everyone close to her with water. Most people laughed, but a few scowled. One lady shrieked. Still, Sheba either didn't notice or didn't care. Confident now that she'd stay with me, I left her leash off her collar and increased my pace to put some distance between us and the others on the path.

Sheba bounded in and out of the woods sniffing everything until she disappeared into a thicket. From where I stood, I could see dirt fly. Shaking my head, I followed.

"Stop that. Bad girl." I tugged her collar.

She yanked free and continued digging.

"Sheba." Ugh. Oh. I froze and stared at a slim hand protruding from the hole Sheba had dug. The bright pink fingernail polish on the hand's nails stark against the dark dirt.

The more my dog dug, the more of the body appeared. I clicked the leash to her collar and pulled her back, tying her to a tree away from the grave. The next thing I did was call Detective McIlroy.

"Yeah?"

"It's Trinity Ashford."

"I know. It's been a few months, but I do know this number. By heart, unfortunately."

"Oh, well then, I'm about to ruin your day. My dog just dug up a body at Waterfall Park. East end of the pond."

"Repeat that?"

So, I did. "It's a little off the beaten path. I doubt others will see, but you might want to hurry."

"Stay there." Click.

I should have brought a snack, but then who knew my dog would dig up a body? I sat cross-legged against the tree where I'd tied Sheba and fought to keep my gaze from landing on the body.

Not long ago, I'd discovered the father of my boyfriend dead in his bed. The discovery had wrenched at my heart. I'd loved that old man and looked to him as a father figure. Waterfall, Arkansas, had once been a quiet small town. At least until big business started arriving. Now, I'd found my second dead body, or at least my dog did, if I didn't count the one showing up at the door of my boyfriend, Brad, that one time.

I mentally counted. Three? Yes, I'd found three dead bodies and almost became one myself.

Hikers passed on the trail on the other side of the brush, oblivious to what lay a few feet away. The body, at least what I could see of it, didn't appear to have been there that long. Southern humidity would have caused decomposition to occur rather rapidly, right?

Hurry up, McIlroy. I shuddered. To top things off, clouds gathered overhead threatening rain. Not how I'd envisioned spending a Sunday afternoon, the only time I really had to myself, since running my own pet store and pet daycare took up most of the week.

A raindrop hit my nose, then another and another. The trees overhead provided little protection. I sighed and crossed my arms around my middle, jumping to my feet when I spotted McIlroy marching down the path.

"In here." I waved.

He frowned and joined me. As I started to show him the partially unburied body, he shook his head. "I can see it." He hunkered down next to the hand.

"How do you find these? It's not a talent most people would want."

"My dog found her."

"Hmmph. Last time it was Armstrong's cat."

I shrugged. "What can I say? It must be a newly acquired gift I have of adopting animals with a tendency to find bodies."

He stepped away and called someone, presumably the police station. The detective seemed oblivious to the rain.

I, on the other hand, felt like a drowned rat. With a wet hand, I shoved my wet hair away from my face. "Can I go?"

"Not until I ask you some questions. You ought to know the routine by now."

"It's raining." I crossed my arms.

"I'm aware of that fact."

I groaned and stood under the thickest tree I could find. Poor Sheba whined and plopped down, resting her head on her paws. Poor thing looked as miserable as I felt.

McIlroy drilled me until I felt as if I repeated myself. I hated being interrogated. "I didn't kill her, Detective. Sheba dug her up." How many times did I have to say those words?

"All right. You're free to go. If you remember anything, saw anyone—"

"The body is that fresh?"

He didn't answer, but the tic in his jaw told me the body had been recently buried. What if I'd stumbled across the killer? I glanced at Sheba. Was she old enough to be protective if someone came after me?

I scanned the area, said goodbye to the detective, and untied Sheba. No walking back to my car for me; I ran.

At my apartment, I took a shower as hot as I could stand it, closing my eyes and envisioning the day's events washing down the drain. After toweling off and getting dressed, I curled up on the sofa with the monstrous mastiff, the one who had started a whole new set of problems for me.

To be honest, I didn't enjoy finding dead bodies, getting involved in solving murders, or almost becoming a victim myself. I drew my legs up to my chest and wrapped my arms around them. Maybe this time would be different. No one other than the detective even knew I'd been the one to discover the body. No one would think I knew a thing, which I didn't. I had absolutely no reason to be nervous.

My cell phone rang, almost bouncing off the coffee table. I snatched it. "Hello?"

"You found a dead body?" My friend and pet groomer, Shar screeched, her voice alive with excitement. "Why do you have all the fun?"

"How did you find out?" I rolled my eyes.

"Mildred Snelling told Mrs. Nelson, who told Mrs. Murdoch, who told me."

"How did Mildred find out?"

"Her son was jogging around the lake, saw the crime scene tape, asked one of the spectators, who said they overheard one of the police officers mention your name."

I sighed. "Actually, Sheba dug it up. Do we know who the victim is?"

"I sure do. News travels fast around here. Oh, I

hope the family has been notified. How horrible to hear this kind of news through the grapevine."

"Shar, who?"

"Oh, right. Sarah Turner, the manager at the Waterfall Trailer Park."

Why would anyone want to kill Sarah? The kind, middle-aged woman had run the trailer park since her husband's death ten years prior. As far as I knew, everyone loved her. "How did she die?"

"Strangled. Tragic."

A knock sounded on my door. "Someone's here. I'll talk to you later."

"Keep me on the phone. What if it's the person who killed Sarah?"

"Why in the world would they be after me?" I frowned but did hesitate before peeking through the peephole. "It's Brad. Bye." I hung up and opened the door. "Hey."

A worried look graced his handsome face. "Are you all right?"

"I guess you heard."

He nodded, guiding me to the sofa. "McIlroy called me. He wanted to make sure you made it home okay. He said you were a bit rattled when you left the scene."

"I was. Especially when I found out how fresh the body was." I plopped onto the sofa. "It brought home how close I'd come to stumbling across the act itself."

"No, Sarah wasn't killed there, just dumped."

I narrowed my eyes. "How do you know all this already?"

"I spoke with one of the new officers, David

Rickson." Brad grinned. "He has a loose tongue."

"Must be the same one who started the grapevine." I hugged a pillow to my chest, grateful all I saw of Sarah was her hand.

He scratched behind one of Sheba's ears. "Good girl. Who knows how long that poor woman would have lain out there if not for you?"

The selfish part of me wished someone else's dog had dug up Sarah. "How was your trip? I missed you."

He leaned over and kissed me. "I missed you, too. Even three days away were too long. It was good. I got the backing to finish the theater."

After Harold Jenkins, contractor and murderer of Brad's father, had been arrested and sent to prison, work on the theater across the parking lot from my shop had stalled, costing Brad money. Folks around Waterfall were looking forward to not having to drive thirty minutes to the nearest theater.

"That's wonderful."

He stood. "Want me to make coffee?"

I nodded. While Brad smiled and made small talk, I could tell something bothered him. If he didn't tell me on his own, I'd ask him to spill whatever it was before he left. "How's Moses doing after you've been gone so long?"

"Needy." Brad laughed. "The complex maid came in a couple of times a day to give him company, but I think he prefers me."

"Should I be jealous?"

"Of the cat?"

"No, silly. The maid." She'd seemed eager to watch Sheba a few months ago when Brad and I were busy finding his father's killer. I'd lived in the penthouse guestroom a few months ago after someone broke into my apartment, thus bringing my pets with me.

"Of course not." He pressed the button on the coffeemaker. "I've got the best girl in the state."

My heart warmed. Never in a million years would I have thought that small-town girl, Trinity Ashford, would be the girlfriend of one of the country's most eligible bachelors. It saddened me to realize it took the death of his father for us to meet.

The delicious aroma of brewing coffee filled my apartment drawing my cats, Sharkbait and Trashcan from their hiding places. I never could figure out why they rushed into the kitchen at the smell, unless they thought coffee meant feeding time, since I usually made a pot first thing in the morning before feeding them.

They immediately jumped on my lap and demanded food. "Silly things, it's afternoon, not morning."

"Here you go." Brad handed me a cup of java made just the way I liked it with a dollop of French vanilla creamer.

"Thanks." I speared him with a sharp gaze. "Now, mind telling me what has you so worried?"

"I'd rather not say."

"Brad—"

He exhaled heavily. "When McIlroy went to the office at Waterfall Trailers, he found every news article written about you after you helped bring down Jenkins scattered across Sarah's desk. One of the articles was pinned to the desktop by a knife."

THE DOG WHO FOUND A BODY

Chapter Two

"Why would Sarah have news articles about me?" My blood ran cold. And why would one be pinned to the desk with a knife?

"The authorities aren't convinced the articles were put there by her." Brad sat next to me.

"You mean she found them in someone else's possession? Who would want to harm me? I haven't done anything to put a target on my back in months." It had to have something to do with Harold Jenkins or Amber Stirling, the woman who pretended to be one man's mistress while helping Jenkins commit murder and fraud.

"I don't know, Trinity, but I don't like it. Not a bit."

Neither did I, to be honest. "I need to go to the trailer park and do some poking around."

"Absolutely not. That's why I didn't want to tell you."

I narrowed my eyes. "You can't keep something like that from me."

"Remember what almost happened with Jenkins? Do you want to go through that again?"

I crossed my arms. "No, but what if someone brings trouble to me? That isn't my fault." If he wouldn't help me stop this before I ended up like Sarah, I knew who would. My good friend Shar.

"Don't be mad because I care about what happens to you." Brad took my hand. "You tend to be impulsive in these situations."

True, but I would go on the offense this time and stop things before they turned ugly. Last time, McIlroy had asked for my help, knowing the residents of Waterfall would talk to me before a police officer. This time I wouldn't wait to be asked.

"What are you thinking?" Brad peered into my face.

"Nothing."

"I know when a woman says nothing, there is definitely something."

A lot of truth in that, but I couldn't tell him I planned to go against his wishes immediately and find out why Sarah had articles about me scattered around her office. Brad and I had only recently become a couple. I didn't want to let go of being the gal on the town's most eligible bachelor's arm.

Brad rested his head against the back of the sofa and groaned. "It doesn't matter what I say, you're going to do what you want."

"Want to watch a movie?" I smiled and reached for the remote, flipping to the cooking channel in hopes of learning a new recipe. I wasn't the greatest of cooks, but I did enjoy trying new recipes to prepare for Brad. Practice makes perfect, right?

His hand entwined with mine, and we watched TV in silence.

The next morning, I blurted out what had been found in Sarah's office the moment Shar and Heather stepped through the door of Tail Waggin'. "Brad doesn't want me to go nosing around, but—" I raised my eyebrows.

Shar plopped her purse on the counter. "How can you not? Someone is following your fame. They must have something against you to kill Sarah."

"But why Sarah and not me?" My shoulders sagged. "I've done nothing to warrant anyone being this interested in me."

"Not true. You brought a scam to light." Shar leaned her elbows on the counter, her gaze locked on me. "Jenkins must have family we don't know about. Someone who would be very upset about his death."

Heather took a deep breath. "I could have Bobby ask around. Now that he's in prison, he might be able to learn…something."

Heather's husband had been involved with stealing cars and reselling them. When danger escalated, he turned himself in, leaving my friend to raise her toddler son alone.

"If you think it won't get him in trouble." The last thing Heather needed was more trouble. As far as that went the last thing any of us needed was more trouble, and here I was making plans to get involved. I needed my head examined.

"What's the plan?" Shar asked.

The arrival of the first grooming appointment, a silver-haired poodle named Sparkles, kept me from telling her I didn't have an idea other than snooping through Sarah's office. Which would have to wait until after work anyway.

Shar carried the hyper ball of fluff to the back after the owner promised to return that afternoon to retrieve him. I booted up my computer while Heather fed and watered the beagle puppies we had for sale.

Trashcan and Sharkbait jumped on the counter, their favorite spot to survey the day's comings and goings. After responding to reservations for grooming and boarding, I smiled and greeted the clients who used our pet daycare services. Once upon a time, I'd wanted to be a veterinarian and also wanted to strangle Brad when I thought he'd raise my rent, thus making school harder to afford. Now, business had grown, thanks to his helpful insight, and I focused on the career I already had as a business owner. I didn't have much time for anything else.

When the rush died down, I made a fresh pot of coffee and gathered Shar and Heather at the small table and chairs near the store window. I could have used the valuable space for products, but after we solved the case of Mr. Armstrong's murder, meetings had become common place, even if all we talked about was what happened in our lives. This morning, we had a different agenda.

After we were seated, I said, "I'm going to the

trailer park tonight. I want to see for myself the articles and the knife holding one to Sarah's desk."

"I'm going with you." Shar lifted her coffee as if she toasted herself.

"Any help from me has to come during the day," Heather said. "The daycare closes at six."

"Not a problem." I blew on my hot drink. "You've already taken on the task of asking Bobby to ask around the prison. With Jenkins being in the same place—"

She shook her head. "Jenkins is in the maximum-security unit. Bobby isn't."

Right. Murder and car theft weren't exactly the same. I shrugged. We might get lucky in finding out something anyway.

"Is Brad coming?" Shar asked.

"No, he doesn't want me getting involved."

"Men. If not for you, he would be dead." Shar shook her head. "I'm kind of hoping to get caught. I haven't had an opportunity to lay eyes on the handsome Detective McIlroy in ages."

Actually, it had been his father's cat, Moses, that had saved us both by creating a distraction. "He's just being protective."

"Yeah, that's what Bobby's excuse was." Heather sprang to her feet. "You two can fill me in on what you find. My husband will call tonight, and I'll ask him to see what he can do. He owes me a lot."

Yes, he did. She'd chosen to stay with him after finding out they were financially broke because of his gambling, which turned out to be the reason he started stealing cars for Mr. Roberts. Of course,

Roberts still hadn't been convicted since he had minions do the dirty work and always had an alibi.

~

Shar showed up at my door seconds after the streetlights came on. She eyed my shorts and tee-shirt. "Why aren't you wearing black?"

"The shirt is black." I pulled the door closed behind me and locked it. "It's too hot to wear long pants."

"But your legs are mayonnaise white. They practically glow in the dark."

I rolled my eyes and followed her down the stairs. "Oh, and the teal Thunderbird doesn't attract attention?" I loved her car almost as much as I loved Brad's luxury Mercedes. "Aren't you afraid of someone vandalizing it?"

"I only worry about that after we've made the bad people mad." She grinned and climbed into the driver's seat.

I'd recently bought a new-to-me SUV since acquiring Sheba who needed a large backseat, but Shar never wanted to let me drive. I clicked my seat belt into place. "Let's go. You know the way?"

"Of course, I do. I carry a map of the whole area in my head." She tapped her temple.

I agreed. My friend did seem to know almost everything about everyone in Waterfall, Arkansas. Which came in handy when snooping into possible motives for murder.

She parked the Thunderbird behind the trailer park office, put the convertible top up, and locked the doors. "Bad people or not, there's no sense inviting someone to steal the car."

"Right. Make them work for it." I grinned, leading the way around the corner toward the office.

Yellow crime-scene tape hung motionless on a windless night. Most of it had already been pulled away, puddling on the ground. Most likely by looky-loos, but I could use that to our advantage if we were caught.

I stepped back and let Shar pick the lock. One of these days I really needed to ask some deep questions about her background. My fifty-year-old friend definitely had secrets.

"Voilà." She used the tail of her shirt to open the door.

"Oh. Here." I pulled some thin rubber gloves from my pocket.

"Thanks. I forgot mine." She clicked on a flashlight, illuminating the darkness. "Wonder who's running this place."

"Owners." I moved around the front counter.

The newspaper articles had been removed. The only evidence left was a hole in the desk where I assumed the knife had been stuck. After pulling on my gloves, I opened the file cabinet on the opposite wall.

Nothing but bills, invoices, and copies of driver's licenses. Not one single article about me.

"Anything of interest is gone." I slumped in the office chair.

"There has to be a reason Sarah was killed. We need to check out her trailer."

"That'll be less illegal, at least." Since no one had strung tape around it. It had me wondering whether the police had stepped foot inside or left it alone because no evidence of a crime pointed to the trailer.

We stepped foot into a trailer with barely enough room to move around. Stacks of newspapers, books, knickknacks, and dirty dishes greeted us. The odor of cat urine almost knocked me out of my shoes. "She has a cat. Here, kitty kitty." Poor thing had to be hungry.

"You don't need another pet." Shar pulled the neckline of her shirt over her nose. "How are we supposed to find anything in this hoarder's paradise?"

"Must be why the police left it alone." It would take a month of Sunday nights to search the place. No time like the present. Somewhere lurked a frightened fur baby. "You look for evidence. I'm going after the cat."

Turns out more than one huddled in the corner of a bedroom. Several cages stacked against a wall held a few more. Anger boiled. Some people did not deserve to have pets. I'd have to call the humane society. Even if I were tempted to take one or two, they all looked as if they needed a vet's services.

I placed the call immediately and started the enormous task of herding the two uncaged felines. After much hissing, a few growls, and fresh scratches on my hands, I had them in cages and started carrying them outside.

I stopped short at the sight of a red-faced Detective McIlroy. "Before you say a word, I couldn't allow her cats to starve to death, now could I?"

"I wasn't aware she had pets."

"So, you hadn't gone in…there yet?"

"Other than a cursory glance, no. Where's your sidekick?"

Knowing he meant Shar, I jerked my head toward the trailer. "I've more cages to fetch. The humane society should be here soon to take possession of the poor cats. What do we do with this place?"

"If she has any family, it'll be their hardship." He shrugged. "Why are you here, Miss Ashford?"

I tilted my head trying to figure out the best story not to get myself in trouble with. "The cats?"

"Is that a question or an answer?"

"An answer?" I flashed a quick grin and hurried back inside to warn Shar. "We're here for the cats, nothing more."

"Got it." She gave me a thumbs-up. "I found other newspaper articles on you and shoved them in my jacket. Maybe they'll shed some light on why Sarah was killed over them."

I grabbed two cages, leaving the last two for Shar, and headed back outside.

As Shar passed him, McIlroy narrowed his eyes. "Why are you crackling when you walk?"

Chapter Three

"Stiff joints." Shar giggled.

"That would be popping, not crackling. Do I need to frisk you?" McIlroy frowned.

"Please do. You'll be the first man in a long time to touch me inappropriately." Shar's laughter increased as she headed for her car.

I rolled my eyes as the detective's face reddened, and I sat on the top step of the trailer to wait for animal control. Why would Sarah keep not one set of news articles on me but two? I didn't know a lot about hoarding, but this didn't seem like something a person would want many of. I wasn't that interesting.

Sure, I'd help bring down a cheating construction boss who also killed people, but other than that, my life was pretty boring. I rested my elbow on my knee and my chin in my hand.

"What's wrong?" McIlroy asked.

"Trying to figure out why Sarah is…was…interested in me."

"It isn't often a small-town business owner brings down a murderer."

I shrugged. "Surely, it happens other places besides Waterfall."

"It does. Don't get involved, Miss Ashford. You might not be as lucky this time." He pivoted and returned to his squad car.

After watching him drive away and making sure he didn't intend to return immediately, I motioned for Shar to get out of her car and come back to the trailer. I didn't want to leave any paper unturned. Get involved? Someone already involved me when they stuck a knife through an article about me.

By the time animal control arrived, I needed a shower from digging through dust-covered stacks of stuff. Sarah had enough magazines and newspapers to fill a history book a few times over.

"You the lady that called?" A young woman stepped into the trailer and wrinkled her nose. "If we're able to save the cats, do you want them?"

I shook my head, wishing I could take them, but my apartment was barely big enough for me, a mastiff, and two cats. "They'll have to be put up for adoption."

She nodded and retreated.

"Anything?" Shar asked from the other side of the room.

"No. I think we're done here." I peeled off my gloves and tossed them in a trash can near the manager's office. "Let's meet up after we clean up and go over those articles."

"Sounds good." Shar drove me home with promises to return in an hour with Chinese takeout.

I stepped over a chewed pair of flip-flops, wagging my finger at Sheba. "Why can't you be good when I'm gone like the cats are?"

Her ears perked up. The dog didn't look the least bit ashamed.

"It's a good thing I only leave my cheap shoes out where you can put your slobbery mouth on them." I patted her on the head and headed for the shower.

The hot water washed away the dust and grime but did nothing to assuage the feeling that danger once again knocked on my door. McIlroy called my not being killed a few months ago luck. I preferred thinking I possessed a bit of crime-solving skill with the help of my friends and fur babies.

I turned off the water and toweled dry, dressed in baggy shorts and an oversized tee-shirt, then went to the kitchen to make tea. Going over the articles with a fine-toothed comb might take until the wee hours of the morning.

Shar's customary rap of two double taps, then one knock sounded at the door. Although I had a peephole, she insisted on a secret knock for my safety.

The delicious aroma of cooked Chinese noodles and sauce teased my stomach as Shar passed on her way to the table. "Can't work on an empty stomach. It's late, but you'll be hungry, mark my words. You're always hungry. I have no idea how you stay so small."

"Chasing after four-legged darlings." I dug into a container of Kung Pao Chicken. Yum.

Shar divided the six papers she'd taken from Sarah's and handed me three. "There isn't a lot about you, but there is some. You didn't make the first page in any but the local paper."

"I wouldn't expect to. Do we know which one the knife had been stuck in?"

"Nope. I'm going to guess whichever holds a clue."

Finding the clue would be the problem since I had no idea what I'd done to be targeted. I flipped through the paper until I found a four-inch column about "Waterfall Girl Brings Down Corruption." It had to have something to do with Harold Jenkins. I drummed my fingers on the table and wondered whether the prison would allow me to visit. Not that he would tell me anything. He'd been really mad as the cops dragged him away.

"What are you thinking?" Shar arched a brow.

"Still believe this is connected to Jenkins. Who do we know that could find out if he has family?"

"Why him? It could be related to Amber Stirling. She was arrested, too."

"Good point. Family?"

Shar shrugged. "Probably. She might be more willing to talk if we have the right bribe. I think we should start with Ladies Night at the club."

I groaned. "I hate that place." The backstabbing, money-hungry women made me grateful to want a simple life.

"That's where information is shared. Bring out your little black dress Monday night." Shar returned to reading the paper. "I heard Evans has a new arm squeeze. She might know something about Amber."

I pressed my lips together. Maybe the country club wasn't such a bad idea. I'd learned a lot in the women's bathroom the last time. "It isn't Summer, is it?"

"No, she went back to the country to start fresh. This one is named Lucy. I've heard she's a knockout. Red hair, voluptuous figure…a man's dream."

"I'd rather go to the gym." I hadn't gone since Summer's stabbing, but it was time to get into shape again. "I don't see anything to warrant killing Sarah."

"Here we go." Shar slid the paper over to me. "The classifieds."

I scanned the page, losing my breath as I read, "Wanted. A nosy pet daycare woman who can't keep her nose where it belongs. Preferably dead."

"That's the first one." Shar handed me another paper.

"Wanted. Pet store owner to give back what was taken."

All six papers had a classified notice. The last paper—the one I'd bet the knife had been stuck in—was the first notice on the page. I glanced at Shar. "Sarah must have figured out who placed these ads. That's why she was killed. Would she have told anyone?"

"That's what we need to find out. We also need to put in an anonymous call to McIlroy telling him to check the classifieds. I've got a burner phone."

"Why?"

"Just in case." She grinned. "This is the perfect time for me to use it." She pulled a small phone from her purse, punched in some numbers, and lowered her voice to a gravely one. "Check last week's classifieds. Each day." She hung up and dropped the phone back in her bag.

"What do you think I supposedly took?" I stared at the notice.

"Someone's freedom? Maybe by sending Jenkins to jail you kept someone from coming into money? Could be almost anything."

"Hmm." Could it really be about money? "I think we should focus on finding out what Sarah knew. Let's head back to the trailer park after work tomorrow and start knocking on doors. She was bound to have had a close friend."

"Don't forget the funeral once the body is released. The killer always shows up at the funeral."

"You watch too much television." I started clearing off the table, stacking the newspapers and sliding them onto the top shelf of my tiny coat closet. If McIlroy found out I had them, he'd confiscate the only evidence I had.

"At least we have a plan. Tomorrow, we visit the trailer park. The next day, the gym. On Monday we dress up and hit the club." Shar grabbed the leftovers. "Unless something steers us in a different direction. See you in the morning."

"Good night." I locked the door after her, then moved to the window to make sure she was safe.

I'd need to tell Brad about the classifieds. He wouldn't be happy, but he'd been there for Jenkins' arrest, too. The danger might not be aimed at just me.

Shar slid into the driver's seat and waved up at me, then sped away with a screech of tires. It amazed me that she'd managed to avoid a ticket with the way she drove.

My gaze fell on the still uncompleted movie theater across the way. Brad told me that construction would resume on Monday with a new company. What if Jenkins had hidden something over there? What if that's what the classified meant? What if someone thought I'd found something hidden?

I sent a quick text to Shar, just in case something happened to me, then clipped a leash on Sheba's collar. "Come on, girl. You found Sarah. Maybe you can find me something else." I clutched a flashlight like a weapon and headed down the stairs and to the theater.

Brad kept the door locked, but I also knew the side exit door never latched properly. I slipped inside and turned on my light.

The boarded windows would provide me with some protection from being seen from the outside. The inside held stacks of drywall, two-by-fours, and cans of paint.

"Come on, girl. Use that nose."

The first thing Sheba found was a half-eaten sandwich covered with mold. Gross. I snatched it up before she could wolf it down and tossed it in a trash bin. "We aren't looking for food."

She peered up at me as if to stay she was searching for something altogether different than what I wanted. I shined the flashlight in my face and gave her "the look." With a doggy sigh, she put her nose to the ground and pulled me along.

I averted my gaze from the top floor where I'd found Amber holding Brad at gunpoint. I'd have to go up there sooner or later and preferred later. Now, if I had something to hide, where would I put it?

The scrape of something in the recesses of the theater made me freeze. Sheba glanced back, but her hackles didn't raise. I relaxed. Mastiffs weren't known barkers, but she'd definitely alert me to possible danger.

She led me toward where a future concession stand would be. I shined the light along the wall and floor, then behind the counter, but I saw nothing of interest. I really wanted to break down a new wall or two, but Brad would have my hide. He was already upset over the delays in construction.

Our next stop, the men's room. No toilet tanks to look in as everything was behind walls. No mirrors or sinks yet. I started to feel as if my idea wasn't such a good one after all.

Something clattered from the front of the building. Sheba made a sound deep in her throat.

A flashlight beam blinded me. "You're snooping without me?"

"You scared the living daylights out of me." I whirled.

Red and blue flashing lights slipped through the cracks in the boards on the window.

"Run." Shar took off for the side door like a rocket, with Sheba and me on her heels.

26

Chapter Four

We raced the long way around the strip mall and thundered up the stairs to my apartment where I collapsed with nervous giggles on the sofa. "That was close."

"I can't breathe." Shar fell into the chair opposite me, holding her mid-section. "Do you think the cops know it was us in there?"

Someone knocked on the door. I sighed and pushed to my feet. "I'm going to say yes."

Since Sheba almost bent herself in half wagging her tail, I guessed it would be Brad on the other side of the door. I was right. A tousled-headed, sleepy-eyed, irritated man stood there.

"Hey, Brad." I stepped back and let him in.

"Hey." He gave me a quick kiss. Probably because he knew he might not be in the mood in a few minutes. "Were the two of you in the theater? I got a call from the police that a silent alarm had been triggered." He kept his gaze locked on me. "Two sets of human footprints and one massive set of dog paw tracks."

My shoulders sagged. "It was us." I rambled off everything I could remember of that evening, including the classifieds. "I thought maybe Jenkins had hidden something in the theater. I knew construction would resume tomorrow, so I wanted to search tonight. When did you set an alarm?"

He ran his hands through his hair, making it stick up even more. "When supplies were being moved in. Trinity, you're killing me. Why do you always have to get involved?"

"What else am I supposed to do? I didn't put those notices in the paper. Now that someone did, I need to find out who before someone else is killed. Obviously, I know something I don't think I know."

"Then I'll help you as I can." Worry creased his face. "I have contacts who can dig into Jenkins' background. Maybe they can dig something up."

"We're going to the prison on Saturday to try and visit Amber," Shar said. Then, she proceeded to tell Brad the other things we had planned. She looked very pleased with herself. "We've got plans."

"Sure looks that way. Can you wait to go to the trailer park until about six? I want to go along as much as possible to try and keep the two of you out of trouble."

"Sure." I grinned. Women couldn't help spilling everything they knew when Brad smiled at them and laid on the charm. I sobered. "Watch yourself. You might be in danger, too. You were with me when Jenkins was arrested."

"I've thought of that. I'll be careful. I know how you value your independence, but if things heat up, I'm going to pressure you to move back into the penthouse for a while."

"Okay, but not yet." I did love waking up to see him first thing in the morning, but staying in his guestroom wasn't as much independence as I preferred. Not ever having had a serious relationship with a man before, I wanted to take things slow.

Shar left at the same time Brad did. My bed had never looked so good. I'd only have five hours of sleep before opening the store in the morning.

~

The next morning, I stumbled blurry-eyed and heavy-limbed downstairs to the store. Bless his heart, Brad stood on the sidewalk with the largest mocha-flavored coffee our local coffee shop sold. "My hero." I climbed on my tiptoes and kissed him. "Do you have a few minutes to sit?"

Once upon a time, his father had brought me coffee every morning, and we'd sit and chat. I'd been the one to find his body after someone murdered him. Brad's obligations kept him from joining me every morning as his father had, but he did as often as he could.

"I have a few." His smile sent my stomach into somersaults. "You look like you need more sleep. Why not have Heather cover for a while?"

"Too many reservations for boarding, and thanks. That's what every girl wants to hear." I smirked and headed for the small table in the corner of the store.

Puppies for sale started barking from inside their cages. I lifted each of the beagles and the Shih tzus out and set them in the playpen. I couldn't do the same with the kittens since the little rascals tended to climb out, but later, I'd replace the pups with bunnies. Since starting to sell baby critters, my business had really taken off. Add in the grooming service Shar took care of, and money problems were lessening. I doubted I'd ever be as rich as Brad, but that was fine by me.

"The plan tonight is to knock on doors and ask questions?" He arched a brow. "You plan on asking outright…what exactly?"

"If Sarah had been acting strange, been obsessed with me…anything that might lead us to something bigger." I took a big drag on my straw. "There has to be someone she might have confided in."

"Hopefully, otherwise, we'll have wasted a lot of time and energy."

Which busy Brad disliked. I agreed, though. Owning a business took up a lot of time and wasting whatever was left over didn't make a lot of sense.

He left when Heather and Shar arrived, and I turned to my laptop. Reservations for boarding multiplied during the summer months when people went on vacation.

Heather listened as Shar filled her in on yesterday's adventure. "I love my son, but I sure would like to go on these snooping events with y'all. But, it would be my luck that I'd be killed and Robbie would end up in foster care until Bobby got out of prison."

I glanced up. "Has your husband found out anything for us?"

"Not yet. Jenkins has a lot of the inmates scared to get close to him. Bobby will keep searching."

"Tell him to be careful. His life is more important. We'll find out what we're missing. It just might take us longer." I couldn't bear the thought of my friend's husband in danger because of me.

"He's being careful." Heather filled the water and food dishes of the pets to be sold. "Maybe I should get Robbie a dog."

"Don't you have enough to do?" Shar's eyes widened. "Robbie's what, three now? That makes him a handful, and you want to add a puppy to the mix?"

"Maybe I'll get a full-grown dog from the shelter." Her brow furrowed.

What promised to become a debate between the two of them was cut short as the first grooming appointment arrived. Sometimes, mediating between my two friends grew old.

A woman being led by a standard poodle approached the counter. "I'm Mrs. Bridges. This is Prince. We're here for his grooming."

"I'll take this beauty straight back." Shar took the leash from the woman's hand.

"Thank you for choosing Tail Waggin'." I smiled.

"Well, the woman who used to groom Prince died."

I widened my eyes and caught Shar's shocked gaze as she headed for the back. "Oh?"

The woman leaned closer. "Sarah Turner was

31

murdered."

"I'd heard that but wasn't aware she did grooming." No way could she do so in her crowded trailer. "Did she have a shop?"

"No, she came to us. She had a van and everything. Called her business Star Puppies." She glanced through the glass window behind me. "I sure hope you're as good."

"I'm certain we'll meet your expectations." Where would Sarah have stashed her van? Did McIlroy know? "Do you know where she was based?"

The woman frowned. "I'm not sure what you mean by *based*. Do you mean where she lived? Waterfall Trailer Park."

I didn't think I'd get anywhere further with Mrs. Bridges. "Prince should be ready for pickup at one."

After the woman left, I drummed my fingers on the desk. If I had a van and no available parking, where would I park it? I did an internet search for places a person could park long term for a fee. Waterfall had one such place. A field a few miles out of town that the owner had converted into a storage unit and RV parking.

"Hold down the fort." I grabbed my purse and dashed to my SUV before the others could ask too many questions.

Luckily the gate was open. I parked in front of a tiny house used as an office and glanced around the field. Three rows of storage units sat on the right. Motorhomes, boats, and miscellaneous vehicles filled the rest.

Pocketing my car keys, I meandered around the

vehicles searching for Sarah's van. Bingo. It sat nestled between two motorhomes. I reached for the door, surprised to find it unlocked.

"May I help you?"

I turned to face a man with crossed arms and a stern expression. "This is my friend's van. She's recently deceased."

"She owes me money. If someone doesn't pay up, I'll have to sell the van."

"Her death is an ongoing police investigation." I crossed my arms, mimicking him. "I'm pretty sure you can't do anything about the van until that is complete."

He tossed me a set of keys. "I don't want any trouble. Take the van."

"I'm willing to pay the cost owed. How much?"

"One forty. Pay that and the van is yours."

I wrinkled my nose, thinking things through. If McIlroy found out about the van and that I had knowingly purchased it during an ongoing investigation, what would he do? I wasn't sure I had the acting ability to get away with it. But, if I didn't take the van, I might lose valuable evidence. "I'll write you a check. Can you hold the van until this evening?"

"We close at five."

I sighed and wrote the check, then drove back to Tail Waggin'. "Shar, when's your next appointment?"

"Noon. Why?" She pulled her feet off my desk.

"I'll explain on the way. I'm driving. Heather?"

"I've got this. Just don't be long." She put the last puppy in its cage and pulled out a bunny. "Sold a Shih tzu when you were gone. I put a blue ribbon in its hair. The owner will be back in a little while. Want me to make up some more care packages?"

"Yes, please. You're a sweetheart." I flashed a grin vowing to find a way to replay her for being my right hand. I'd already given her a raise but wanted to do something more personal.

As I drove back to the van, I explained everything to Shar. "Since I can't drive two vehicles at once, I need you."

"You bought a van for one-hundred and forty dollars?"

I laughed. "Yep. As soon as I told the manager the van might be part of a police investigation, he couldn't wait to get rid of it."

"Makes you wonder what he might be hiding, doesn't it?"

My mouth fell open, then clamped shut. "I hadn't thought of that. What if he's the one who killed Sarah?"

"We need to get inside his office. Feel up to another nighttime excursion?"

"Not really. I'm exhausted from the last one, but yes." Brad and McIlroy were going to have heart attacks. "First, we search this van thoroughly, then let McIlroy know about it. We'll get it back once they find Sarah's killer."

"And I can do grooming on the weekends in my spare time."

Just like that, she took over my van. I sighed and pulled into the lot. "I'm not exactly sure what my plans are for the van."

"If the grooming service becomes mobile, you

can expand the front of the store, knocking out that one wall. You're getting kind of cramped."

I handed her the van keys. "Good point. I'll think on it when it's with McIlroy."

The manager marched toward us. "That was fast. I'll be glad to be rid of the thing."

Shar batted her lashes as she did with every man close to her age. "Glad to be of service, and sorry our friend's van was so much trouble, bless her soul. Did you know her, too?"

"Not outside of this place." He hurried back to his office.

"Rude man." Shar exited my car and climbed into the driver's seat of the van.

I sure hoped I knew what I was doing by buying the thing.

Chapter Five

The rest of the afternoon passed with people browsing for pet supplies, when in reality they wanted to ask questions about me finding Sarah. For the umpteenth time, "My dog dug her up. I wasn't looking, just hiking."

David, the man who delivered my supply orders, leaned on the desk. "You must keep your boyfriend worried out of his mind." He grinned, his teeth flashing against his dark skin. Once upon a time, David had incessantly asked me on dates, but once word spread about Brad and me spending time together, he dropped the matter, content to be my friend.

"Hey, gorgeous." Shar sashayed past us. "If I were only thirty years younger—" She waved a hand in front of her face as if she were hot.

David laughed. "If I could only get that lucky." He straightened. "Be careful, Trin. You might not be my girl, but I don't want anything to happen to you."

"I'll protect her," Shar said.

"I'm sure you will." With a salute, he headed back to his delivery truck.

Why wasn't it five o'clock yet? I itched to search that van before heading to the trailer park.

Mrs. Nelson entered the store, her schnauzer, Greta, on a leash instead of a carrier. "My sweetie is out of vitamins."

"You bought some last week."

"Fine. I heard you're the one you found Sarah's body."

Here we go again. "Sheba did."

"That monstrous dog?" She cut a sideways glance to where Sheba, for once, lay still. "She's only a baby."

"With a nose for trouble." I sighed.

"Have you thought of hiring a trainer?" She tilted her head. "You might want to before she's too big. Now, back to Sarah. We went to school together, you know?"

"No, I didn't."

"She wasn't very popular. Too nosy. Head of the school paper and always butting into other people's business."

Ah, that might explain why she collected all the articles on me. She probably considered me a local celebrity. "Why would someone want to kill her?"

She shrugged. "Probably dug up some dirt on them."

Which I'd already figured out. When another customer entered, I excused myself and joined the woman in front of the puppy cages. "May I help you?"

"I'd like a beagle for my husband's birthday. They're good hunters, right?"

"Yes, ma'am. Male or female?" They were easily identified by the pink and blue ribbons around their necks. Once fresh and new, they now hung in shreds from roughhousing.

"I'll take that little boy right there."

I removed the one she chose, overjoyed when a new fur baby found a home. After ringing her up, I handed her a care package. "Enjoy. He's a sweetie."

More curious people who didn't buy anything meandered in the shop, and finally the clock showed five o'clock. I quickly turned the sign to closed.

"Eager?" Heather grinned. "I'll clean up. You and Shar go snoop."

I gave her a quick hug. "You know me so well." I took Sheba with me and Shar to keep guard. She'd alert us if anyone other than a friend tried to approach the van parked in the alley.

Holding out my hand, I wiggled my fingers. "Keys."

Shar dropped them into my palm. "I could have unlocked the door."

"I'm too excited. We're going to find something, I know it." A selfish part of me wanted to be the first to enter. I unlocked the panel door and slid it open.

Where Sarah's trailer had been cluttered from junk, the van was spotless. Grooming tools hung from a pegboard. In one corner of the back lay a coiled water hose with an attachment for washing animals. Glassed-in shelves held shampoos, fingernail polish, fragrance, and ribbons. I couldn't imagine a single thing that Sarah might have missed having, and the cleanliness of the place didn't leave a lot of hiding places. On a small counter sat a laptop.

"Wow. You got a bargain for your money." Shar whistled. "I sure hope McIlroy returns this quickly once he takes possession. I'm sold on the idea of a being a traveling groomer."

I wasn't, but I hadn't taken a lot of time to think about her suggestion. I grabbed a handle on the frame and hauled myself up. "Don't mess up anything."

"Okay, Miss Bossy Britches." Shar followed me into the van. "I'll check the glove compartment. It's a bit obvious, but we can't not search."

Trying to find information on someone we didn't know the name of, who might have found a reason to target me and kill Sarah, would be almost impossible. It made sense to me that such information might be on paper or a Jumpdrive. With my hands on my hips, I turned in a slow circle, searching for places to hide one or the other.

A ring in the floor revealed a pull-up grooming table. Clever. I placed it back down and turned to the shelf of supplies. Other than that, I couldn't think of anywhere to hide something except in the front seats or in the walls.

First, I tried peering behind the shelves for a place big enough to slide a sheet of paper. Nothing. Firmly bolted to the wall. I even searched inside the water hose. "Anything?"

"Nada." Shar called from the front. "Except a roll of cash."

"What?" I whirled. "How much?"

"A lot. All hundred-dollar bills. The glove compartment isn't a very safe place to keep money."

"Do you think she was bribing someone?" I hadn't considered that possibility at all.

"Keep looking."

I turned back to the supplies, reading the labels. One seemed more faded than the rest. A faint X had been scratched across the face. I opened the cabinet and retrieved the bottle.

Something rattled inside. My heartrate increased. Here was something. I removed the lid and turned the bottle upside down. A Jumpdrive fell into my palm.

I quickly booted up the laptop and inserted the device, emailing the files it contained to my computer. As the clock ticked toward six and Brad's arrival, I didn't have time to give them even a quick glance.

Once the files were sent, I replaced the Jumpdrive in the bottle and put it back on the shelf, then rushed to make sure none of the files remained on Sarah's laptop. The more digging I did, the more laws I broke. I intended to tell McIlroy about the Jumpdrive in the bottle if he caught us but not that I'd sent the files to myself.

Sheba started whining outside.

I shot a startled gaze at Shar. "Put the money back."

While she did, I retrieved the bottle and the

Jumpdrive.

"Get out of there." McIlroy's deep voice sent my heart into my throat. He tapped on the passenger side window.

Shar opened the door and slid out. "You really need to ask me out to dinner so we can talk about your surly attitude."

"Out, Miss Ashford."

"You do know she owns this van, don't you?"

I stepped out to greet a shocked McIlroy. "I guess you didn't know."

"Since when?"

"This afternoon." I pasted on the biggest grin I could. "Got it for a steal because Sarah owed payments to the storage unit place. Did you know she had a side business?"

"Yes. This van is evidence. I didn't expect to find it in the alley."

"Why are you in the alley?" I asked.

He shook his head. "I always park back here when I go to the shops. You never know who you might see doing something they shouldn't."

"Oh." I handed him the bottle. "I found this."

"Shampoo?" His eyes widened as he shook the bottle.

"And there's a lot of money in the glove compartment." Shar crossed her arms. "You're welcome."

"For what?" He frowned.

"For us doing your job." She patted his arm. "Well, we've other things on our agenda. See you later."

"Wait a minute."

"Yes?" Shar and I said in unison.

"Why did you go to the storage unit to get this van? I realize it wasn't difficult to find out Sarah had a grooming business—"

"Right," I said. "A customer mentioned it. Then, I thought it might be a good idea to take over her—"

"That was my idea," Shar interrupted. "I want to be a traveling groomer."

"I don't care whose idea it was." High spots of color appeared on McIlroy's cheeks. "You're snooping into my investigation. Where's the keys?"

"Will I get the van back once the investigation is over? I need to get the title transferred." I handed him the keys.

"Unless you make me mad enough to drive it into the lake, you will. I'll have Officer Rickson pick up the van." He turned and stormed down the alley to his squad car.

"That man definitely needs softening up." Shar shook her head.

"He's probably a lot nicer when he doesn't have to deal with amateur sleuths."

"Good point. Let's go look at that Jumpdrive."

"We don't have time. Brad will be here soon. The trailer park awaits." I took up Sheba's leash and headed around the building and up the stairs to my apartment, leaving Shar to follow.

"I doubt we'll find anything as exciting as what we did in the van."

I agreed. We'd hit pay dirt. I'd be up late again poring over the files on my computer.

By the time I'd fed my three fur babies, Brad

arrived.

"How was your day?" He wrapped his arms around me and gave me a kiss that sent electricity through my veins.

"Not bad." I smiled up at him. "You're in a good mood."

"Construction has resumed."

Right. I'd been so busy with nosy customers, I hadn't glanced across the mall parking lot.

"You seemed to have been busy."

I nodded. "Sold a puppy and bought a van."

His brows shot up. "I can't wait to hear that story."

I explained about Sarah's business and how I came to be in possession, concluding with Shar's idea of expanding my business and McIlroy confiscating the van temporarily. "Remember when I thought you were going to ruin me by raising my rent?"

"How could I forget? We butted heads at every turn." He chuckled.

"The exact opposite has happened. You improved this strip mall, gave me some ideas on how to increase my finances, and things have shot forward so fast my head is spinning."

"All you needed was some encouragement." He took my hand. "Are we ready?"

"If the two of you are finished with the gushy talk, yes." Shar stormed past us. "We're wasting daylight."

Laughing and still holding hands, Brad and I followed, locking my door behind us. "Want to look at a Jumpdrive I found in Sarah's van when we get home?"

Brad's smile faded. "You found something already?"

"That and a bunch of cash. All of which McIlroy will have, but yes, we found something already." Feeling rather pleased with myself, I slid into the front seat of Brad's Mercedes, leaving Shar in the back.

Chapter Six

We were going to find Sarah's killer quicker than we brought down Jenkins. I could feel it in my bones. After all, we'd already found a Jumpdrive. Brad and I would pore over the files later tonight, plying ourselves with cups of coffee to keep us fueled. I chuckled to myself. That seemed to be what most of our "dates" consisted of. Coffee and crime.

Brad parked next to Sarah's trailer and peered through the front windshield. Yellow crime-scene tape waved like an eager child who'd seen their friend. "Good thing you went in already. Want to start with the first trailer, split up, or what?"

"Since someone is already watching Trinity," Shar said, "I vote for staying together."

"Good point." I shoved open my door. "We'll start on this side and go up the other until we're either finished or it's too dark." I didn't think folks would answer their doors after dark, and since it was summertime, dark didn't come early. We had plenty of time.

No one was home at the trailer next to Sarah's. If we had time, we'd stop by later. At the next house, an elderly woman answered the door.

"If you're selling something, I don't have any money." Her wrinkled face broke into a smile. "But, I've got lots of time if you're seeking something else."

"Thank you." I stepped forward. "We're actually here about Sarah. Did you know her other than as your manager?"

"Everyone knew Sarah, but not everyone liked her. She did monthly checkups on the properties, making sure trailers and yards were kept exactly as stated in the rules." She gently pushed a Yorkshire Terrier back from the door with her foot. "Some say she was too picky. Me...well, I kept to the rules, so when she came to my door, we spent a few minutes chatting."

"About anything that might point to why someone would want her dead?"

"Are you police officers?"

"No, ma'am." Brad shook his head. "Just friends."

"Ah, yes. This young lady found her body."

I sighed knowing I'd be forever known from here on out as the woman who found dead bodies. "My dog did."

"Semantics. Anyway, I don't know who would have killed Sarah and buried her body in the woods. I'm sorry." She lowered her voice. "The man in number twelve hated her with a passion. You might want to ask him."

"Thank you, we will." I turned and led the way to the next trailer. We struck out on one trailer after another. Sarah hadn't been well-liked, but no one knew of anyone who would kill her. I stopped in front of number twelve. "Here goes nothing."

"What?" A burly man in a stretched-out tank top stepped onto his small porch before we reached the trailer. "I've seen you going door-to-door. I ain't got time for the census, and you ain't carrying a briefcase. You one of them religious zealots?"

Brad took the lead on this one. "We're here about Sarah Tur—"

The man spit and said something too nasty to be repeated. "Got her just desserts if you ask me. Always nosing around, taking pictures, leaving notices. I'd say she saw something she shouldn't, and someone knocked her off."

"Who?" I blurted out.

"If I knew that, I'd tell the cops, not people I've never laid eyes on." He stepped back into the house and slammed the door.

"I didn't see any pictures in her trailer," Shar said. "Do you think we missed them?"

"It would have been easy to overlook them in all that stuff." Unless McIlroy had them.

"They might be on the Jumpdrive," Brad said. "That's where I'd keep them."

"But Sarah kept hard copies of all the newspaper articles. I'm betting she has prints of the photographs." I glanced in the direction of her trailer, itching to go back inside. "How much trouble would I get into if I crossed that tape?" Not that I hadn't before, but McIlroy had already given me warnings.

"If we find the photos and turn them over, all will be forgiven. I know it." Shar marched toward Sarah's trailer.

"Hold on." Brad reached out and grabbed her arm, stopping her. "Just tell McIlroy our suspicions. Trust me. Any photos, if they exist, will be on the Jumpdrive."

"Which he has." I nodded. "Okay. We've wasted enough time. Let's not risk arrest. We have plenty of other people to question."

By the time we finished, dark had settled over the town. Other than the man in number twelve, we learned nothing more than the residents of the trailer park were worried about who would replace Sarah. Better the devil they knew than the devil they didn't, many said.

How sad to have been so disliked. I stared out the passenger window as Brad drove us to my apartment. Wait a minute. Where was Sarah's camera? What if there were photos not downloaded yet?

"We have to go back and find her camera."

"That means crossing crime scene tape," Brad said. "Are you sure?"

"Yes. I'll go in myself. You and Shar be the lookouts. Better yet, act like you're knocking on doors and have no idea what I'm doing."

Brad snorted. "Like anyone will believe us."

"Do you have a better idea?"

"Yeah. Don't get caught." He turned around on

the shoulder of the road and sped back toward Sarah's trailer. "You search the trailer. I'll search her office."

Good. I didn't want to be the only one to risk arrest, but on the other hand, I didn't want my friends to get in trouble. "We'd best hurry before someone calls the police."

Shar handed us each a small flashlight. "I'm always prepared. You'd be amazed at what all I carry in my bag."

"Not really." I grinned and rushed toward Sarah's former home.

It took an hour, but I emerged victorious, having found the camera in a box that had once held Pop-Tarts, shoved way back in the refrigerator. Sarah sure liked to hide things in plain sight. I stepped out of the trailer, box in hand, and glanced around the park.

A dark shadow skirted around the building that housed the office. I bit back a shout of warning, instead, hunkering over and making haste to warn Brad and Shar.

"Someone's outside," I hissed.

They both jerked up from their searching and clicked off their lights.

"Stay here." Brad gave us both a stern look. "I'll check it out. If I'm not back in ten minutes, call the police."

I clutched the hem of his shirt. "We should stay together."

"It'll be easier for me to sneak around if I'm alone." He cupped my face. "I'll be back. I promise."

I nodded, praying this was a promise he could keep. Then I grabbed Shar and pulled her behind the cover of the desk as Brad stepped outside. Keeping my eyes on my watch, I stared as the minutes ticked down.

Brad returned in eight minutes. "I didn't see anyone. That's our cue to get out of here."

We rushed back to his car, this time returning to my apartment.

"I've got a nine o'clock grooming session tomorrow," Shar said. "So, rather than be a third wheel, I'll be going. But—" she waved a finger in my direction. "I want to see pictures tomorrow."

With promises to print off any of interest, I watched her leave, making sure she made it to her car safely. Someone knew we'd been snooping around Sarah's whether we'd caught them or not.

"Jumpdrive or SIM Card first?" Brad booted up my laptop.

"Since the files from the Jumpdrive are already uploaded, let's start there." I sat at the kitchen table next to him, cradling Trashcan in my lap. Poor babies. I'd been gone so much lately.

We scanned photo after photo of weeds growing around trailer skirts, undriveable cars parked in the road, and a few stray animals which I wanted to rescue and put up for adoption. There were a few of a smiling Sarah at different events around town, one of which was the dedication of the theater.

Roberts, the owner of the local used car lot was there, Jenkins was there, Evans, the man who owned the gym next door...everyone who was anyone in Waterfall had attended the dedication.

Sarah had snapped photos of them all. My heart ached a bit at her obvious dream of working for the local newspaper in some capacity and not having time to fulfill that dream.

"I'm not seeing anything that should have gotten her killed." Brad exhaled heavily. "Let's check the SIM Card." He pulled it from the camera and inserted it into the laptop.

"Bingo." The word came in a harsh whisper.

On the screen were photo after photo of men stealing cars. One of them was Heather's husband, Bobby. The liar. He obviously knew more than he was letting on. "Who is that?" I pointed at a man standing in the shadows.

"Let me zoom in." Brad moved the mouse around the enlarged photo. "I can't tell. It's too dark."

"Is that Roberts' mechanic garage?"

"I don't think so. It's too large. Looks more like a warehouse. No, it's a barn."

"Any idea where it is?"

"There are hundreds around here." He sat back in his chair. "I can't see any identifying features of the man watching. The only person clear is Bobby Langley."

I continued to study the photos, printing them off as I clicked on each one. "Shar knows the area well. Maybe she'll see something we're missing. Hold on. It looks as if the man in the shadows is wearing glasses." Roberts didn't wear glasses that I knew of.

"Too dark, unless they're sunglasses. Look at this one. Sarah zoomed in close." Brad tapped the printer photo. "It looks like there are gold cufflinks on his wrists and a gold chain around his neck."

This was hillbilly country. Not many men wore jewelry, but then again, a lot had changed after the rich started buying up property. "It isn't much to go on."

"No, it isn't." He rubbed his hands down his face. "It's midnight. I need to go home and see to Morris, then get some sleep."

"Shar and I are going to the gym after work tomorrow. Want to meet us there?"

"Sure." He gave me a quick kiss. "Put these photos somewhere safe. I'll think of a way of getting the camera and SIM Card to McIlroy. Don't want to be guilty of withholding evidence. We're in enough trouble as it is by going under the tape. I'll think of something to appease him."

I chuckled. "Better you let him know what we've done than me. He likes you more."

Brad tapped my nose. "Because I don't annoy him every time he turns around. Lock the door."

After he left and the door lock clicked into place, I leaned my back against the smooth steel. Exhaustion coated me, but my brain worked overtime. Who was the man in the photo, and how could I persuade Bobby to tell me? I didn't want to endanger him, but I needed to know the man's identity.

My gut told me Richard Roberts was the man in the photo, but proving it wouldn't be easy. When I'd snooped around a few months ago, Roberts had warned me to stop snooping. Had that been for his own protection or for Jenkins'? The two had been friends, but maybe what I'd chalked off to friends protecting friends hadn't been what happened after all. Maybe I'd been close to finding out whatever Sarah had discovered.

Instead of making me feel better, the knowledge sent a shiver down my spine. If he was the killer, I'd gotten in his way twice. Roberts would definitely be aware of my involvement in the arrest of Jenkins. The target on my back just grew larger.

Chapter Seven

Shar and Heather studied the photos I'd printed off the night before. When Heather recognized her husband, she waved her arms and paced like a mad woman.

"You're scaring the puppies," Shar said, frowning. "If you must throw a fit, do it outside."

"He's been lying to me." Heather deflated into a chair. "When I threaten him with divorce, he makes all these promises to get me to back down."

"Do you want a divorce?" I raised my brows.

"Of course not. I took vows." She groaned. "I don't see that I have any other choice. The danger to my son grows with each lie his father tells me."

"What are you going to do?"

"Tell Bobby about the photo."

"No!" Shar and I yelled in unison.

"No one can know about these or we'll end up in a hole like Sarah." I shook my head. "This is our secret. Clues to help us find out who wants me out of the picture. Don't tell Bobby anything." I turned back to the pictures. "Brad thinks this is in a barn. Shar, do you recognize anything?"

"Woodpecker holes." She tapped the photo. "That's why the sun comes in round. That building probably looks like swiss cheese. With all that light, that's why Bobby is easily identified and the other man is in a shadow."

Ah, I could see what she meant. The sun streamed in over the shoulders of the man in glasses, giving us his silhouette and very little else. "Finding a barn full of woodpecker holes will be near impossible. There must be a lot of them."

"Drive down any country road, and you're bound to see a few." Shar turned, shielding me from her first appointment of the day.

I scooped the photos into a pile and slid them into my laptop bag. "Good morning, Mrs. Smith. How's Ricky?" I smiled at the squirming white fluff that made up her bichon frise.

"Energetic. He loves coming here."

"Must be the tender loving care we give." Shar took the pup from its human. "I'll have him ready by noon."

"No hurry. I have errands to run." She waved her fingers in farewell and left the store as Brad entered, his hands full of cardboard cups of coffee.

"Sorry I'm late. Overslept." He handed each of us the drink we favored, even going into the grooming area to hand Shar hers. When he returned, he gave me a tender kiss on the cheek. "Anyone recognize anything in the photos?"

"Only that it's a barn full of woodpecker holes and Heather wants a divorce."

He glanced to where my friend still sat at the small waiting table. "Understandable. Her husband has caused her a lot of hardship and heartbreak."

My heart ached for my friend. I wanted to take away her pain but knew the best thing I could do was be there for her. "What's on your agenda today?"

"Blueprints to go over to improve on some of Jenkins' work, then things should move rather quickly. He accomplished a lot before his arrest. I want to make sure we fix any corners he cut. Meet you at the gym at five?"

"See you then." Ugh. I'd never been a fan of the gym and even less now after I'd been stuck in a dark shower while two stalls over, someone was being stabbed. Thankfully, Summer had survived and gone back to Oklahoma.

David arrived with a dolly of boxes and placed them just inside the door. "Hey, girls. Find any more bodies?" He laughed as if he'd said the funniest joke in the world.

"Very funny. Let me sign for those and you get out of here." I wiggled my fingers for him to hand me the electronic gadget in his hand. "You aren't funny."

"I thought so." He snorted and bent to pet Sheba who lay next to the counter, tail thumping. "She's grown bigger every time I see her."

"Know of any good dog trainers?"

"Sure, I do. Mabel Lawrence lives out on 105. She's great with animals." He scribbled directions and a phone number on the Post-it Notes I kept close at hand.

"Thanks." I'd make the call that afternoon. The darling scamp had chewed up another pair of shoes last night, not to mention digging up a potted plant I'd managed not to kill. Hopefully, it would recover in its refilled pot of dirt.

It often occurred to me that Sheba's tendency to destroy things might have been why I'd found her in the middle of night. Someone else had given up on her.

I spent the rest of the day picking up the slack from my morose friend, Heather, spraying out empty kennels for new boarders and periodically checking emails. Because I dreaded five o'clock that day when I usually looked forward to the time, the day sped by.

I trudged up the stairs to my apartment and pulled out one of the two workout outfits I'd bought from the thrift store a couple of months ago. If I had to sweat, I might as well look cute.

Donning the black knee-length pants with a yellow stripe down each leg and a tank top that matched the stripe, I pulled my hair into a ponytail and grabbed my gym bag. Just in case the women's shower was out of soap and towels, which they wouldn't be, since Brad paid for me to be a Platinum member, but I liked being prepared.

"Don't look like you're walking the green mile." Brad took my bag. "Walk the treadmill, watch TV, and keep your eye out for anything suspicious. I'll be doing most of the snooping since we're probably looking for a man."

"You don't think a woman is involved?"

"I'm not ruling it out, but my gut tells me it's a man working alone." He opened the door to the gym next door and waved at the receptionist.

Shar already jogged on one of the treadmills. I chose the one beside her and set a water bottle in the holder before turning on the machine. While we ran side by side, I told her of Brad's theory.

"Men are often influenced by women."

"Not in Jenkins' case."

"Mark my words. If Roberts is the bad guy, either his wife or his mistress knows."

I stumbled and almost fell. "He's married?"

"Well, they don't live together, but they've never divorced. Something about a prenuptial in the wife's favor."

Very interesting. "Does Mrs. Roberts attend women's night at the club?"

"Not that I know of. She's a homebody." Shar increased her speed. "Orders groceries online, anything to stay safe in her mansion."

"Where?"

"Outside of Little Rock. Want to pay her a visit?"

"Not unless we're sure it's Roberts. Don't want to scare any possible suspect away. I want indisputable proof so justice can be served." I increased my speed a bit. Sweat tickled its way down my spine despite the fact I only walked at a fast pace.

Shar looked me up and down, laughed, and put earbuds in her ears. She might be more than twenty years older, but she put me to shame in the fitness department.

Just as I started to put my own earbuds in, a Marilyn Monroe-type with red hair sashayed past. Every male turned to stare except Brad. He glanced up from lifting weights but returned his attention immediately to the task at hand. I smiled.

Shar reached over and nudged me. "That's Lucy."

Oh, Roberts' new mistress. I hopped off the machine and followed her to the thirty-minute workout area. I wouldn't strike up a conversation unless she did but wanted to watch her for a while to get a hint as to what type of woman she might be. Other than a married man's mistress, that is. I didn't think I'd ever understand how a woman could give herself to a man for prestige and money.

Lucy cut me a quick glance, then watched the light over our heads for the cue to start the first exercise. I chose the second so we could both do the workout without getting in each other's way.

She'd hit the showers when we finished, and I'd follow her. It would mean not finishing the rotation, but that didn't bother me in the slightest. My dilemma was how to speak with her in a friendly manner and find out if she knew about Roberts' suspected illegal activities. Nothing came to mind on how to approach the subject.

"Aren't you Brad Armstrong's girlfriend?" Lucy asked as we waited for the next rotation to start.

"Yes. Why?" I wiped my brow with the small towel hanging around my neck.

"You don't look the type."

I frowned and started to ask for clarification, but the light turned green. When we stopped again, I asked, "What does that mean exactly?"

She shrugged. "No offense, but you look small-town."

"I am small-town." My frowned deepened. "That shouldn't matter one bit."

"Don't get angry. I'm surprised is all." On to the next machine.

I worked out my frustrations on the stepper and bit my tongue in order not to say anything unkind. Too bad others didn't have the same manners. My control only lasted until the next one-minute break.

"Aren't you Richard Roberts' arm candy?" I tilted my head. "You are aware he's married?"

"Separated."

"Semantics."

She laughed. "I've hurt your feelings. I apologize."

Shrugging like it didn't matter, I planted my feet against the bar in front of me and waited for the light to turn green. Shar would say the woman was jealous because I had Brad. I thought maybe she was trying to find out where I stood socially.

When she headed to the showers, I followed, faltering inside the door.

Lucy arched a brow. "What's wrong?"

"Last time I entered these showers, someone was stabbed."

"By you?" She took a step back.

"No. By another man's mistress." I flashed an evil grin and punched in the combination to my locker. Opening the door, I pulled out a robe and headed to a shower stall, avoiding the one where an attempt had been made on Summer's life.

Lucy didn't enter the shower room. Had I frightened her? Tipped her off? Time would tell.

Knowing that I might have sent her running to Roberts, I took the fastest shower ever and hurried to the main part of the gym to wait for Shar and Brad. Shar waved on her way to the locker room. A few seconds later, Brad joined me.

"Learn anything?"

"That the fancy women don't think I'm good enough for you." I crossed my arms. "Other than that, no."

Chuckling, he unfolded my arms and pulled me closer. "It's I who am not good enough for you, my sweet Trinity. None of those women can hold a candle to you."

I smiled, knowing I'd never cared about such things before. "They definitely aren't good enough for you."

"What the heck?" Brad shot to his feet and darted outside, me right on his heels.

His Mercedes sped by.

"This is the second time my car has been stolen."

"Maybe it won't end up in a pond this time." I slipped my hand in his.

"What if I don't get it back?"

"Insurance?" I glanced in front of Tail Waggin', relieved to see Shar's T-bird still there.

A young man ran his hand over the hood, caressing the T-bird as if it were his recent romance. He circled the car, then jumped into the driver's seat and gripped the wheel. When he bent over, Brad and I sprang into action.

Brad yanked him from the T-bird so roughly before he could hotwire it the guy rolled across the sidewalk and into the grass. "Who took my car?"

"I don't know." The young man held up his hands.

"Who do you work for?"

"I don't know that either. I get a text telling me where the car is they want taken. When the car shows up at the drop site, the money is deposited in my account."

Brad pulled him up by his collar. "Where's the drop site?"

Chapter Eight

"Dude! Relax. The drop site is the Lucky Star motel on 64." He slapped at Brad's hands.

"What happened?" Shar joined us.

"Someone stole Brad's car, and this guy tried to steal the Thunderbird," I said.

Shar immediately slugged the poor young man with her bag and called him names I couldn't repeat. When Brad tried to hold her back, she kicked out, hitting Brad instead of her target.

"That's enough." I wrapped my arms around her middle and pulled her back. "The car is still here, and Brad is trying to get information out of the guy. Don't knock him senseless."

Brad scowled. "Instead of being hysterical, do something useful, like calling the police."

Shar fought free of my hold. "I'm checking out my baby."

After fishing in my gym bag for my phone, I

called the police. When I told them we had one of the thieves in custody, they promised to be right out.

Brad pushed the young man to a sitting position on the curb. "Move and I'll break your leg."

"Got it. Geez. I'm just trying to make a few bucks."

"By stealing cars." He frisked the man, found a cell phone, and pocketed it. "Wouldn't want you to alert anyone. Will my car be at the motel? For how long?"

"They park the cars among those renting rooms. It's usually a few hours before someone is dropped off to drive the car to wherever they take them."

I thought the guy knew more than he was telling, but other than torture, I doubted we'd coerce him to tell us everything.

Lucy exited the gym, sending us a curious glance before heading across the parking lot. She didn't appear to know the young man, but I'd met good actors before.

"I'll take Shar to the motel. We'll see if your car is there and keep an eye on it if it is. That way, it's ready for you when you're finished with the police."

Brad tossed me his keys. "Drive it back if you find it."

"Drive your car?" The beautiful Mercedes with the butter soft seats? I grinned. "Gladly."

He chuckled and snaked an arm around my waist, giving me a quick kiss. "Be careful. You're more important than the car."

"I'll be careful." Feeling as if I'd been given a

great gift, I told Shar the plan.

"Good. If I see someone try to drive off in Brad's car, I'll beat them."

Of that I had no doubt after the fury she unleashed on the poor guy left with Brad. "We're going to retrieve the Mercedes, nothing more." I climbed into the front passenger seat.

Seconds later, we sped toward the motel. Old, but clean, it barely survived after the interstate moved in. But, the Lucky Star was a monument to the 1940s where Hollywood stars, singers, and musicians traveled through here on their way to bigger things. Now, the motel was just a cheap place to rent a room and get a simple continental breakfast.

The Thunderbird fit right in place in front of the vintage building with flashing neon lights, spraying color over the tan walls of the motel. My gaze searched the lot, finally landing on Brad's Mercedes parked under a broken streetlight. "There."

Shar parked at the other end. "I'm not leaving until we see who comes for the car. They'll know for sure who hired them."

"True, but the police might arrive before them, and we'll have sat here for nothing." I shoved open my door. "I'm at least going to get close enough to stop anyone who tries to drive away."

"Fine by me. Oh, goodie. They have a soda machine outside. I wouldn't mind one. Want anything?"

"Diet, please." I headed for Brad's car. Where could I watch without being seen myself?

A few people came and went, but since the

motel didn't have a pool, no one lingered outside. Shar and I would be noticed right away. "Can you find out whether the room in front of the Mercedes is available? If so, rent it. We can watch the car without being seen that way."

Shar nodded and handed me the diet soda. "Sometimes you're smarter than I give you credit for."

"That's not very nice."

She laughed and headed for the manager's office, returning a few minutes later with the room cards. "Here we go." She unlocked the door and waved me in.

Two queen-sized beds covered with neutral tan duvets took up most of the room. I'd expected orange and green paisley and felt pleased that someone had renovated the place. I pulled a chair from a small corner table and placed it in front of the window. Parting the curtains just enough to peer through, I waited.

Shar reclined against the bed pillows, turned on the television, and browsed channels. "Doesn't take two to peek out. Let me know if anyone comes."

"I thought I'd keep that information to myself."

"Smart aleck." She sat up. "Did I do something to make you mad?"

"You told me I was stupid."

"No, I didn't." She swung her legs off the bed.

"Yes, with your remark about me being smarter than you thought." I narrowed my eyes, daring her to lie.

"That was a joke." She laughed and returned her attention to the television. "I'm sorry if it was in bad taste."

"Thank you." I turned my attention back to the parking lot. A few seconds later, I snapped my fingers. "Someone is approaching the car."

Shar rushed to my side. "It's a girl."

"Girls can drive, too."

"Where did she come from?"

"The woods across the road, I think." Or maybe up the road. I'd been arguing with Shar instead of watching.

The girl glanced toward the motel just as Shar parted the curtains a tiny bit more. She whirled and dashed down the road.

"Good job." I got to my feet. "I doubt the thieves will send anyone else. We might as well return the car to Brad."

"Sorry. My fingers have a mind of their own." Once we stepped out of the room, leaving the card keys on the dresser for the maid to return, Shar glanced at the corner of the mall. "Camera. That will have picked up the girl's face."

My mood brightened a bit. "I'll follow you back." She'd pass and leave me in the dust if I didn't. This way, she had a clear road ahead of her.

As usual, I caressed the leather seats of the Mercedes. Buttery soft. The interior smelled of Infamous, the cologne that helped me solve my friend's murder, all because a cat detested the scent. Woodsy, musky, with a touch of spice…I loved it.

With a sigh, I turned the key in the ignition and followed Shar from the parking lot. It didn't take long for her to pull ahead, but I could still spot her taillights. No way would I speed and risk wrecking

Brad's baby.

I reached over and turned on the radio. Country music blasted from the speakers. How did I not know that my suit-wearing boyfriend liked country?

With the empty road stretching out before me, the temptation to take the long way back almost overwhelmed...wait a minute. Empty road. Darn it, Shar. I didn't know the area the way she did.

We'd turned left onto the highway, then taken an access road...the one I just passed. Now, I'd have to find a way to backtrack. The joy of driving the Mercedes started to drip from me and puddle at my feet. The longer I had the car, the greater chance of me doing something to it.

Headlights appeared behind me, blinding me as I glanced in the rearview. *Go around, idiot.* Instead, the vehicle drew closer. A large black truck filled the back view.

Despite my reluctance, I pressed harder on the accelerator. The truck did the same.

Fear choked me. Was I about to be kidnapped? Was it me or the car that attracted whoever's attention? Maybe it was just kids out playing games? I preferred that scenario. If so, hopefully, they'd get bored and go away.

The truck rammed my back bumper. I fought to keep the wheel steady. The next ram of the truck snapped my head forward. *Please have another vehicle show up.* I hated the fact that I was alone at night on an unfamiliar road with a maniac slamming the back of Brad's car.

I risked increasing my speed again, then whipped the wheel to the left, spinning to face the opposite direction on the other side of the road. I sped back the way we'd come. By now, tears blurred my vision. I wasn't normally a crybaby, but under the circumstances, I couldn't be too hard on myself.

My phone rang. I debated the danger of driving one-handed while I dug it from my pocket and chose to answer the call. Someone needed to know where I was. The call ended before I could answer. I hit redial.

"Where are you, sweetheart?" Brad's voice made my tears start to fall.

"I don't know. Shar drove away too fast. I missed my exit. Now, someone is trying to run me off the road. I'm heading back in the direction of the motel, but I'm not sure where to turn." I started blubbering. "Your car is banged up."

"How are you? Are you hurt?"

"Not yet."

"Stay on the road. Do not stop driving. I'm sending help."

I glanced at the gas gauge. Almost full. "Okay, Hurry." I hung up in order to focus all my attention on the road.

Hope leaped in my chest at the sight of headlights approaching. Finally, I was no longer alone.

The truck rammed me again.

Shar drove past, mouth and eyes wide.

I screamed as the car fishtailed. This wasn't a fight I would win.

The driver of the truck seemed undeterred, even as Shar turned around and followed. Of course, anyone with half a brain would know that the owner of a mint-condition vintage car wouldn't ram another vehicle. All Shar could do was follow and keep a watch on me. I'd take all the help I could get, no matter how small.

Another ram, the hardest yet. My body lurched against the seat belts. The Mercedes sped off the road, down a steep ditch, and into a tree. Airbags exploded with the force of a train, knocking the breath from me. I coughed and fought to extricate myself from the bags.

I unfastened my seat belt, but no way was I opening the door. If I wanted out, it would be through the shattered front windshield. And I did want out in the worst way possible.

My head pounded, the pain increasing as I used my gym bag to clear the glass from the window. Coming toward me was the silhouette of a man. I had to get free and hide.

From the road, Shar blared her horn in what I guessed was an attempt to distract my pursuer. It didn't work. He kept coming closer.

My phone. I glanced around. Where was it? The floor.

I bent and screamed as pain shot through my ribcage. Whatever adrenaline had kept the pain at bay was drifting away. Stretching my hand out for my phone, my fingers snatched it up. I straightened to see the most wonderful sight in the world. The flashing red and blue lights of a squad car and my pursuer racing for his truck.

I leaned my head back, closed my eyes, opened my mouth, and cried long and loud. I'd regain my composure tomorrow. Tonight, I'd let out all the pain and fear. Then, I'd get mad, and somebody would pay.

Chapter Nine

"Trinity!" Brad's voice jolted me out of my crying fest.

I opened my eyes to a tongue-washing by Sheba. "Off, you big oaf." I shoved against her, stopping as pain ripped through me.

"Are you all right?" Brad pulled the dog away and peered through the window. "Anything broken?"

"Your car." I sniffed.

"I mean you." He turned away. "Help me get her out."

"The door won't open."

"I know, sweetheart. We'll get you out." He reached in and gripped my hand. "Hold on."

"I'm not going to die, but something is definitely broken." My guess was a rib or two. "Did you catch the guy who ran me off the road?"

"He got away. Everyone is more interested in

you right now."

"Miss Ashford?" McIlroy took Brad's place. "How are you feeling?"

"Like I rammed into a tree. Why don't y'all get me out of here before asking questions?"

It seemed like an eternity before the fire department arrived and freed me from the Mercedes. Brad insisted I be carried on a stretcher to the waiting ambulance. "I'm going with you. Let me give Sheba to Shar."

"Why did you bring Sheba?" I asked when he joined me in the ambulance.

"She's good at finding bod…uh, I figured she'd use her nose if you took off into the woods."

"Nice save." He brought the dog to help look for my body. Thank God, I was still breathing, although every breath hurt. "Sorry about your car."

"Don't be. It's insured. Maybe I'll buy a junker that nobody wants. This is the second time my car was stolen."

"No. I love the luxury of the Mercedes." I smiled. While I had never cared much for the lifestyle of the rich, I'd grown accustomed to being spoiled a little since meeting Brad.

McIlroy met us at the hospital but waited until I was placed in a curtained-off room before bombarding me with questions. "Did you get a look at who ran you off the road?"

"Just his silhouette when he started into the ditch. He drove a big truck."

"What about at the hotel? See anyone?"

"A girl, maybe twenty, maybe younger. Caucasian, dark hair, wearing jeans and a yellow hoodie. Shar moved the curtains on the window and she ran off."

"You were on surveillance?" His brow furrowed. "I thought you went to retrieve the car."

"We did, but I thought we could catch a glimpse of the thief."

"Look where that got you." He shot an exasperated glance at Brad. "What were you thinking letting these two knuckleheads retrieve your car?"

"That I was the better one to watch the thief." Brad glared and crossed his arms. "Trinity wasn't supposed to stay."

"Hey. I can make my own decisions," I said, rolling my eyes like a teenager.

"Good evening. I'm Doctor Meyers. Mind if I take a look at our patient?"

I'd never been so glad to see a doctor in my life. I was in no mood to play referee.

The doctor asked the two men to wait outside, then called a nurse in. "Heard you had an accident?" He placed a cold stethoscope against my chest. "Where does it hurt?"

"All over, but mostly my ribcage."

"We'll need x-rays. You'll have some pretty colors showing up within the next few days. Seat belts tend to bruise with an impact like that." He shined a light in my eyes. "Mild concussion. Did you hit your head?"

"I might have on the window, but I don't see how. The car had lots of airbags."

You've a small bump on your forehead."

Ah. I must have hit it on the steering wheel

during one of the rams from the truck, but I was too frightened to notice.

An x-ray confirmed cracked ribs. A few hours later, Brad called for a ride and took me to his penthouse. "No arguing. I'll make sure the pets are brought here tomorrow, but you need to be looked after, and this is easier." He helped me into the guest bed. "Plus, there's security here."

He didn't need to tell me that another attempt might be made on my life. "But I'm supposed to go to the prison with Shar on Sunday."

"Doesn't look as if that'll happen for a few days." He tenderly kissed the bump on my forehead. "Yell out if you need anything. I'll hear you."

The aroma of frying bacon and brewing coffee woke me the next morning. I groaned getting out of bed and padded to the kitchen as if I were a hundred years old.

"Why are you out of bed?" Brad turned, spatula in hand. "I would have brought you breakfast."

"I'm not an invalid, and I'm going to be late for work."

"You're not going to work."

"Yes, I am. I need to feed the animals and retrieve my vehicle." A couple of bruises and cracked ribs wouldn't keep me down. I had a killer to find before I became the next victim.

"Why are you so stubborn?" Brad narrowed his eyes.

"Why are you so bossy?" I glowered.

He stared at me for a minute, then laughed. "I think we're having a fight."

"Really?" Neither of us had raised our voices.

Didn't fighting mean yelling? "Not a disagreement?"

"Maybe. I can handle this kind of argument." He turned back to the stove as I carefully lowered myself onto a kitchen chair.

A couple of minutes later, coffee and a plate of eggs and bacon sat in front of me. "Thanks."

With his own plate, he sat across from me. "I tend to get bossy when I'm worried, but I care about you, Trinity, and I'm more than worried at this point. You could have died last night."

"That's why it's imperative I find out who killed Sarah before they succeed with me." I picked up a slice of bacon. "It's past the point of me sitting back and doing nothing. That ended with the knife pinning a newspaper article to Sarah's desk."

"I know," he said softly. "But I will be worried the whole time and will rarely let you go anywhere without me. I'll take you to work if you promise not to lift anything. You'll be safe with Heather and Shar there. But, I want you sleeping here. After work I'll follow you. No more driving anywhere without backup."

"Yes, sir." I saluted him. Since he'd agreed to let life continue for me outside the penthouse, I wouldn't be too irritated that the bossy tone had entered his voice again.

I took a sponge bath, then went back to the kitchen to wash my hair in the sink. I'd no sooner bent over to let the water run over my scalp when Brad arrived.

"I'd love to wash your hair." He poured shampoo into his hands and massaged it into my scalp.

I struggled to breathe, and it had nothing to do with my ribs. I bit my lip to stifle a groan. The gesture of him washing my hair was the most sensuous thing I'd ever experienced. A delicious shiver skipped down my spine as Brad pressed his lips against the back of my neck.

"A soft kiss will have to do," he whispered, his voice hoarse. "What I'd like to do won't be good for your ribs."

Mercy. My eyes popped open. Shampoo ran into them, burning.

"I'm sorry." Brad chuckled, all romance gone, and handed me a towel for my eyes.

Had he been teasing me? I turned, flinging water from my hair over the front of him. Calling his bluff, I asked, "What, exactly, were you wanting to do?"

His gaze fell to my lips. "Kiss you with all the passion that goes with realizing I almost lost you."

"Oh." My lips parted.

"I'll be gentle." He lowered his head.

A pounding on the door broke the spell. I didn't know whether to be relieved or upset at the interruption. While I wanted his kiss, very much, I agreed that things could get carried away and I'd be hurting.

Brad opened the door to let Shar with Sheba on the leash inside.

"I could have brought Trinity to work."

"I'm here to hand over this menace." Shar handed him the leash. "She chewed up a pair of expensive heels." She glared at me. "When are you going to get her trained?"

"I meant to call the other day. Remind me at work. Bad dog."

"Because of her tendency to chew, I didn't bring the Thunderbird. You can tie her in the bed of my truck." She narrowed her eyes. "Why are the two of you all wet? Is that shampoo? Did I...Oh, I interrupted something." She laughed. "I'll be downstairs when you're ready."

My face heated as if I'd been in the sun all day, I quickly rinsed the shampoo from my hair and shuffled to the bedroom to change into dry clothes. I chose to put my wet hair in a ponytail rather than dry and style. Fifteen minutes later, I joined Brad in the living room.

"I'll walk you down." He crooked his arm.

I slipped mine in, then took up Sheba's leash.

Brad matched his steps to mine, taking care not to jar me. Sweet, but I'd already moved around more than the doctor would have approved. It didn't matter. The ribs weren't broken, just cracked. I'd live, and the pain wouldn't last forever.

"Don't drive her crazy as you normally do, please," Brad told Shar as he helped me into her truck. "She doesn't need jostling."

"I'll drive like an old lady." She grinned and started the truck. "Just like you worry like an old man."

"Ha ha." Brad stepped back.

I waved out the window. "Thanks for picking me up, Shar."

"Didn't want responsibility for that beast for one more second. I can see why someone dumped her."

"Now, you know it's never okay to dump an animal. Besides, she'll outgrow the bad behavior in a year or so."

"Then let her gnaw on your shoes." Shar kept her word and drove the speed limit. She reached over and patted my leg. "I'm glad you aren't dead."

"That's nice. Me, too." I smiled.

She parked in front of the store, then rushed around to help me out. "I promised your man that you would do as little as possible. You go right in and sit down at the counter. Heather and I will take care of everything else. I called her last night and filled her in on the accident."

Heather was on her cell phone when we entered. The look on her face led me to believe she didn't like what she heard. When she hung up, she took a deep breath. "Bobby said the car thefts are going to get worse because a competitor is trying to take over."

"Who?" I moved to the chair behind the counter.

"He doesn't know. Said it's the word on the yard, but no names."

Roberts had competition. Waterfall only had twenty-seven-thousand residents. How many sought-after cars could it have? Of course, the nearby towns would add to the choices. "Maybe they'll start fighting and knock each other off."

"Maybe," Shar said, "but what if we get caught in the middle? Now we have two potential suspects to find."

"If we can confirm that Roberts killed Sarah,

we'll put a stop to this." I booted up my laptop. "Do we have somewhere to put a brother and sister Great Dane pups? Ten weeks old. The owner said she's sold the rest but doesn't want to leave them at home while she's at work. Wants us to sell on consignment."

"If we put them in the puppy pen." Heather unfolded the metal circular gate. "I doubt we'll have them long. Put a notice in the paper, and they'll be a quick sell."

A bang on the window alerted me to the morning paper. I'd subscribed after finding Sarah's copies, wanting to stay up on the classifieds.

Shar fetched the paper and handed it to me. Worry creased her face. "I haven't checked the papers before today."

"Neither have I." I opened to the classifieds. My mouth dried up like winter leaves. "Wanted: Foolish woman who knows how to drive without plowing into a tree. Urgently seeking. Would like a face-to-face meeting."

"Well." Shar's brows rose. "That's pretty forthright. Looks like this guy isn't going to let up."

Which is why I needed to bring him down first.

Chapter Ten

"Wanna go with me to look at a new car?" Brad asked Sunday afternoon. "I'm tired of renting."

"Sure, but Sheba has a dog training lesson at one." I glanced up from scouring the morning's newspaper. So far, no classified targeted me.

"How about I drop you off, run some errands, then pick you up at two? It doesn't last longer than an hour, does it?"

I bristled a bit at his insistence to accompany me everywhere I went but also knew the foolishness of going anywhere alone. I was definitely caught between Brad and a hard place, or so they say. "That works for me." I closed the paper and clicked on Sheba's leash.

Sharkbait and Trashcan barely glanced up from where they lay with Moses. Seems being reunited with their murderer-finding friend was more important than giving me the time of day. "Bye, boys."

Sheba strained against her leash toward the elevator. It took all my strength to prevent her from ripping the leash out of my hands and taking off.

"Want me to take her?" Brad reached around me and pressed the button for the elevator. "She's getting too big for you."

"That's another reason for the training." That and I'm running out of shoes."

Mrs. Bridges, the dog trainer, lived on at least ten acres of pastureland a few miles from the city center. A sprawling red-brick ranch house surrounded by a white fence looked postcard beautiful.

The trainer, a short, round woman wearing one of those pointed Asian hats, stepped off the porch to greet us. When Sheba again strained against her leash, Mrs. Bridges pointed and in a soft, but firm voice, said, "No."

"How did you do that?" Hope for the future rose.

She patted Sheba's head when she sat. "This beautiful girl wants to please. She'll respond better to treats and positive affirmation than she will to scolding. How old is she?"

"I have no idea. She was a stray, but she's massive."

"She is a big girl." The woman looked at my dog's teeth. "Less than a year. Maybe six to eight months. Not too late to learn proper behavior. Follow me."

"Good luck." Brad blew me a kiss. "See you in

an hour."

Keeping a firm grip on Sheba's leash, I followed Mrs. Bridges to the back of the house. Several dogs barked from their cages but hushed when she raised her hand. "I'm impressed," I said.

"These naughty darlings stay for a few days. They're being difficult, but they'll come around."

I eyed a pit bull as we passed. I swear the dog's head was as big as mine.

Mrs. Bridges stopped several yards away from the cages. "Now, let's teach Sheba to obey a few hand signals. Each time she gets one right, give her a treat. You do carry some in your pocket, don't you?"

I shook my head. "I'm more used to cats."

Rolling her eyes, she fished some treats from her pocket and handed them to me. "This is only until she's trained. Otherwise, she'll get too fat. The occasional treat is fine, but you don't want her focusing only on them indefinitely. Hand me your shoe."

Plopping on a plastic chair, I removed my shoe and watched in horror as she laid my favorite sneaker in front of Sheba. When Sheba took it in her mouth, Mrs. Bridges removed the shoe, said a gentle no, and set it back down. When Sheba stopped trying to chew on it, she got a treat.

"What about when I'm not home?" I tilted my head.

"She'll need to stay with you or in a crate until she can be trusted."

"A cage?" My poor baby.

"It isn't the end of the world." She sat next to

me while Sheba watched us with big dark eyes. "She needs to learn to sit until told to move." Mrs. Bridges smiled. "You might want to encourage her in the body-finding department."

I shuddered. "She isn't a bloodhound. Guess there isn't anyone around that doesn't know my dog found a body."

"Probably not." Mrs. Bridges laughed. "Mastiffs are fiercely loyal. She'll do anything to protect you. Pat your thigh. If she doesn't come, say come while patting your thigh. No need to say the words loud."

By the end of the hour, I was as exhausted as my big fur baby. "Thank you. I fell in love with this big galoot the first time I saw her and really want her to fit in with apartment life."

"She needs regular exercise. Remember that. I'll see you next week." She turned to the dog cages as Brad pulled into her driveway.

"How did it go?" He climbed out and opened the door for Sheba who sat and stared up at him. "Go on." She leaped up. "Wow, after only one day?"

"She learned no and to sit until told otherwise. I'll have to practice with her, but I'm very encouraged." I smiled as he hurried to open the door for me. "Are we going to Roberts Automotive?"

He laughed. "Maybe. I will not buy anything from that man, but it won't hurt to nose around a little. I plan on purchasing another Mercedes."

Oh, good. "What happened to staying out of the investigation?"

"That was before someone tried to kill you." Jaw set, he closed my door. When he climbed into the driver's seat, he said, "If Roberts is the culprit, we want him to be on the alert, same as we are."

What a turnaround. While it pleased me that my getting run off the road had riled Brad as much as it had me, I didn't want him in danger. In fact, I'd prefer to find Sarah's killer alone so no one I cared about could be harmed. I might want that, but it wasn't feasible.

I read books, I watched the crime shows on TV. Killers went after those you loved in an attempt to keep you from bothering them. No matter what I did, Brad would be targeted. What I didn't understand was why me? If Robert did kill Sarah, then why target me? What was buried in my mind?

"I can hear the wheels spinning." Brad reached over and entwined his fingers with mine.

"Trying to figure out why someone wants me dead. That was easy with Jenkins. We pinpointed him as the killer. I realize Sheba dug up Sarah's body, but the killer could have left me alone. I didn't know anything until you told me about the articles in her office."

"We'll keep searching for clues. One step at a time, sweetheart. That's all we can do."

"There isn't much to go on other than the photo of Bobby and who we suspect is Robert."

"It's a start." When we pulled into Roberts Automotive, I asked, "What's the story?"

"I'm shopping around, unsure whether I want to buy new or used. How are your ribs?"

"Tender but not bad enough for me to stay in the car." I shoved open my door and retrieved Sheba, determined to put some of her training to good use.

Then I glanced around the lot. "Doesn't look as full as usual."

"Maybe there's truth to him having competition."

"Then where are those cars sold?"

He glanced at me. "I don't think any of the cars we see are stolen. Roberts must sell them to someone else. It would be too risky to keep them here."

True. I should've known that. Dogs didn't like to sleep where they went to the bathroom. Same with thieves. Take your dirty business somewhere else.

Keeping a firm grip on Sheba, I strolled alongside Brad, peering at vehicles for sale. I spotted two salesmen, but no Roberts. "Maybe he isn't working today."

"I'm hoping he isn't. I'd like to question the people who work for him." Brad grinned as one of the salesmen approached.

"In the market for a new-to-you car?" The salesman's nametag identified him as Michael Watson.

"Possibly. Not sure if I want used or new." Brad thrust out his hand. "Brad Armstrong."

"I hope I can help you, Mr. Armstrong. See anything that catches your eye?"

Brad shrugged. "Is this the only dealership in town? I heard there was a new one."

The man's smile faded. "Not that I know of, but if there was, you wouldn't find a better deal on a used car than here." He stared at Sheba who sniffed his shoe.

My gaze followed his. Dirt had settled in the crevices of his black shoes. I bit the inside of my cheek, trying to compose my face before raising my head. Was this the man who had buried Sarah's body?

I snapped my fingers to distract Sheba. If he was, I didn't want him suspecting that my dog had sniffed him out. "I'm going to take her for a walk."

What if someone other than Roberts killed Sarah? What if he didn't know an employee of his had done the deed? Or...he could have ordered her killed, thus keeping his hands clean. Either way, I needed to find out if Michael had been in the woods that day.

Brad whistled to catch my attention, and I led Sheba back to him. "You have been a very good girl." I bent and gave her a hug, then offered her a treat.

"How did you get away?" I glanced to where Michael watched us.

"I told him I still wanted to look around and pretended to be interested in that SUV at the end of the line. I might buy it anyway. It's a four-wheel drive. Doesn't hurt to have two vehicles."

Not if you could afford to. "Did you see his shoe? Sheba was really interested in the dirt caked on the sole."

"Yeah?" He arched a brow.

"I'm thinking he might have buried Sarah. And, his body build is the same as the man who ran me off the road. Drive around back. Let's see if there's a big dark truck parked in the employee lot." I climbed into the passenger seat of my car.

Brad waited to answer until he was sitting in the driver's seat. "That's a good catch but a long stretch."

"I know, but after Moses's reaction to Jenkins' cologne, I've learned to trust my animals."

He laughed. "Here we go again."

"What?" I gave him a playful punch. "You can't deny your cat's part in catching Jenkins. Dogs have great noses. Sheba would remember the scents around Sarah's body. We should pay attention to Sheba."

"Fine." Still laughing, he drove past a wide-eyed Michael to the back of the building. "I hope he thinks we're merely turning around." He drove down one aisle and up the other.

"There it is." I pointed to a jacked-up Ford. "I bet if forensics studied the truck bed, they'd find traces of Sarah's DNA."

"Are you sure it's the same truck?"

"Stop in front of it." When he did, I climbed out and studied a scrape on the bumper. I'd bet my best pair of jeans this was the same truck. I returned to my vehicle. "I'm positive. It has scrapes and dents of the type obtained in ramming another car. Can't tell paint color because it's black like yours."

"This brings us a step closer, doesn't it? We need to let McIlroy know so Michael doesn't get away."

"Too late."

Michael sped from the car lot in a cute little sportscar.

Chapter Eleven

"Go after him!" I clutched Brad's arm.

"Your car will never catch that sporty one." Brad shook his head. "We can at least give McIlroy the guy's name and what he's driving."

It was better than nothing but not near good enough. I wanted to put this case to rest before someone else died. "Look. There's Roberts." My hopes rose as the owner of the dealership drove onto the lot. "We can speak with him."

Brad turned the car off. "I doubt we'll learn anything, but it's worth a try."

Keeping a firm grip on Sheba's leash, I followed Brad into the showroom, doing my best to march rather than shuffle. I wanted to look brave, confident, not in pain. Which, if I was honest, I was, though I didn't dare mention it. Brad would take me straight home with an "I told you so."

"We're here to see Mr. Roberts," I told the

woman behind the desk.

"I'll see if he's here."

"I know he is because we saw him drive in." I pasted on what I hoped was a pleasant smile. "Please let him know that Mr. Armstrong and Ms. Ashford are here to speak with him."

Pursing her lips, she reached for her phone. After relaying my message, she glanced up. "He'll be out in a minute."

"Thank you."

A minute turned into twenty before a fake-smiling Mr. Roberts joined us. "How may I help you?" He rubbed his hands together. "In search of a new car?"

"We'd like to speak with you about one of your salesmen," Brad said. "In your office perhaps?"

Roberts blinked a few times, then nodded. "I hope one of my employees wasn't inappropriate." He turned and led us to an office at the end of a short hallway. Once inside, he sat behind a maple desk and waved us toward two chairs. "Please, sit and tell me what this is about."

"What do you know about Sarah Turner?" I arched a brow.

He leaned back in his chair. "I thought this was about an employee of mine, not a murder victim."

"We believe the two are connected." I met his steely glare. "My dog seems to think Michael Watson buried Sarah's body."

He laughed. "Your dog. That thing shedding all over my carpet pointed out one of my men as the woman's killer? Thanks for the laughs, Miss Ashford, but I'm sure you're mistaken."

"Are you aware he drove away in one of your cars after I identified his vehicle as the one that ran me off the road?" I tilted my head. "Don't you think that's suspicious behavior?"

Mr. Roberts stood. "I'm a busy man. If you'll excuse me, I must insist you leave now. What my people do on their own time is none of my business."

"Thank you for your time." Brad thrust out his hand. "Sorry to have bothered you." After Roberts returned the handshake, Brad rushed me to my car.

"That was a waste of time." I shoved my seat belt into place.

"Not really." Brad smiled. "While you grilled the guy, I watched his body language. He gritted his teeth a lot and took sharp breaths through his nose. He knows more than he's letting on. Now, he knows we suspect one of his men. Roberts will make a move and, hopefully, we'll catch him before he kills one of us."

I liked that plan. "Awesome. Now to buy you a car."

We drove to the nearby town of Blytheville. The Mercedes dealership was as different from Roberts Automotive as it could be. Impressively built in glass and concrete, the showroom reigned over the lot like a king surveying his kingdom.

Inside sat shiny new cars in a variety of colors. I wanted to run my hands over the leather interior of each and every one.

Brad approached the receptionist desk. "I'm here to test-drive a Mercedes CT5."

"Yes, you must be Mr. Armstrong." The woman

smiled and handed him a set of keys. "The white car in spot B2 is available. If you decide you like it, we can have your car off the showroom floor and drivable in a matter of minutes. You chose the Smoke Metallic, correct?"

Brad grinned. "I did. The test-drive is just a formality."

"You'll need to leave the dog with me. She'll be fine, but we don't allow pets in the show cars." She held out her hand for the leash.

Praying my pup would behave, I handed her over. I bent to give her a hug, whispering in her ear, "Don't embarrass me."

The receptionist gave Sheba a dog bone, which immediately made the woman my mastiff's best friend. "We'll be just fine."

I had to hold my arm tight against my ribs in order to keep up with Brad's eager pace. Guess I'd be excited, too, if I was about to purchase such a luxury vehicle. I slid onto the passenger seat and caressed the leather seats. "You should buy a new car every year just for the new car smell."

"That's too much money, even for me." He leaned over and kissed me. "Where to?"

"The beach?"

"That's ten hours away."

I shrugged. "You asked."

Chuckling, he pulled from the parking spot and headed for the freeway. "Whoa." He slowed, then whipped the car into the parking lot of a superstore. "There's the car Michael drove."

"How do you know?" And how in the world did he spot the car from the road?

"I memorized the license plate."

"You saw that from the road?"

"No, I spotted the red car, then drove in and saw the license plate. Are you okay?" He looked at me as if I'd sprouted a second nose.

I huffed. "Let's go get him."

We headed into the store. I followed Brad as he strolled the main aisle looking both ways. "There he is." I spotted our prey in the tobacco line.

Michael spotted us and darted out of line, heading for the front doors.

Brad shot after him, leaving me to follow at my slower pace. By the time I reached the door, Brad waited in the car in front of the store, the engine idling. "Come on!"

I shrieked as Brad raced from the parking lot before I had my seat belt in place. God, please don't let us crash. All the fear of my accident rose, threatening to choke me. My breath came in gasps.

"Breathe, sweetheart." Brad cut me a quick glance.

"Eyes on the road." I clutched the safety handle to the right of my head as he sped through a red light.

Once away from the store, amidst honking of angry drivers, Brad followed the sportscar onto the interstate and pressed the accelerator harder. Despite the danger of our situation, a big grin stayed glued on his face.

"You're enjoying this?" I felt as if I'd have a heart attack.

"This car is made for speed. Relax. I'm a good driver."

Maybe, but what about the other drivers? What if someone pulled out in front of us? I squeezed my eyes shut and concentrated on breathing. The blare of a semitruck's horn had them open again.

The red car shot for the next exit.

Brad yanked the wheel to follow, almost missing the exit, and taking us bumping across a grassy patch between the interstate and the exit. If my ribs weren't aching before, they sure were now. I hissed against the pain and pressed my arm against my side.

"I'm sorry." Brad eased off the gas.

"Don't you dare slow down. I'll be fine. Just catch up to him." What he could do then, I had no idea. "I'll call McIlroy and let him know where we are so he can send someone to intercept."

"Excellent idea."

I dialed McIlroy and told him what had transpired that day. "Can you send help?"

"You're telling me that you and Armstrong are involved in a high-speed car chase after someone you suspect is a murderer?" His voice rose several decibels before he finished his sentence. "Are you crazy?"

Obviously. A person had to be a bit insane to get involved in murder, right? "Yell at us later. Are you sending help?"

"Yes." Click.

"He's mad."

"He usually is where you're concerned." Brad leaned forward, peering through the windshield. "He turned off somewhere. Help me look."

Thankful for something else to help keep my

mind off the fact we could crash, I stared out my side of the car. "Back up. I saw a sharp turn. He must have turned off there."

Brad stopped on the shoulder. "We'll have to let the police take it from here. I don't want to risk damage to this car and have to purchase it instead of the one I really want." He punched the steering wheel.

"How'd the car handle?" I put a hand on his arm to distract him.

"Like a dream." He grinned and leaned over to give me a lingering kiss. "We'll wait for the police unless Michael comes out of hiding. Then, the chase is on again."

I selfishly hoped he'd stay hidden. I'd rather catch him in a way other than rocketing down the interstate and side roads.

The rookie, Officer Rickson, arrived about fifteen minutes later and parked his squad car behind us. He approached the Mercedes and rapped on the window. "Got away, did he?"

"We believe he went down that road," Brad said. "This is a borrowed car, so I didn't want to pursue."

Rickson wrote down the description of the car and the license plate. "I'll see if I can find him, but I'm sure he's flown the coop. You two be careful and leave the investigating to the professionals." He slapped the top of the car and hurried back to his.

Which left us to return the borrowed car. The receptionist walked around the vehicle, her eyes narrowing. "You really did test it, didn't you? Usually, folks don't keep the car for an hour or run it almost out of gas."

"Sorry about that." Brad flashed his handsome grin. "I'm willing to sign the papers on the other car, if you want to have someone help us with that."

"How was Sheba?" I looped the leash around my wrist.

The woman's pleasant expression returned. "Everyone loved her, employees and customers. The manager is thinking of purchasing a dog for the store."

"How about a Great Dane?" I told her I owned a pet store and had a male and a female available.

"I'll let him know. Follow me."

I gave Sheba a kiss on the top of her head. "What a good girl. You might have helped me make a sale."

Her tail wagged in response. Smiling, I followed Brad inside.

A few minutes after he signed a check for the new car, Sheba and I were headed home with Brad following behind. All in all it had been a good day.

We'd dug up a clue, didn't die in a fiery car crash, and Brad had a vehicle again. I sobered a bit remembering Brad's remark that Roberts would now make a move. If I wasn't careful before, I'd have to be doubly alert now. In my gut I knew that Roberts wouldn't confront me face-to-face or do his dirty work himself. No, he'd send someone else, and that meant I wouldn't know they were coming.

Chapter Twelve

After an uneventful week, thank goodness, I felt well enough on Saturday to accompany Shar to the prison. Heather, bless her heart, said she could manage the store. I hoped so. Weekends were often busy, not with grooming but with shoppers.

Since Shar didn't want to put a lot of miles on her Thunderbird, I drove the two hours to the prison. A long, lonely drive since my friend figured it was a good time to catch up on some sleep. As for me, my mind kept dwelling on Sarah's murder.

There'd been no more notices in the classifieds. Did that mean we'd scared off the person writing them? Was that person Michael Watson? Or was it Roberts who simply waited for another time to play his games? Of course, it could be someone we hadn't discovered yet. That frightened me more than anything.

It was highly doubtful Amber would have anything to tell us if she did agree to speak with us. I still thought all this had to do with Jenkins, but the pieces weren't fitting together.

When I pulled onto the exit to the women's prison, I nudged Shar awake. "Up and at 'em."

She wiped the drool from the corner of her mouth with the back of her hand and pulled down the visor to straighten her hair. "I feel so much better."

At least one of us did. My eyes were still a little gritty from getting up at the crack of dawn.

I parked the car as close to the prison as I could, then approached the chain-link fence surrounding the building. I pushed the button and stepped inside a fenced "hallway" of sorts. The door closed behind us and I pressed another button for the next door to open. Inside, I strode to the desk where an officer sat and smiled. "We're here to see Amber Stirling."

The officer pressed some keys on his computer. "I don't see any prior approval for any visitors."

"What do you mean we need prior approval?"

"All visitors must file paperwork and submit to a background check. No one has applied to visit Amber Stirling."

"What if I can get a law enforcement officer to vouch for me? Will you bend the rules just once if I can?"

"Who would that be?"

My smile widened. "Detective McIlroy from the Waterfall police department."

"Never heard of him."

My smile started to feel forced. "We came all

this way."

"Fine. I'll call him." The officer placed the call. "Detective, I have a..." he glanced up. "What's your name?"

"Trinity Ashford and Sharon Lee Carpenter," Shar said, bending closer to the officer.

The officer's eyes narrowed, then he handed the phone to me. "He wants to talk to you."

"What hairbrained thing are you doing now?"

I held the phone away from my ear to spare my eardrums. "Helping you. Amber might know something."

"You aren't content to stir things up in Waterfall? You have to spread trouble? Hand me back to the officer."

Grimacing, I handed the phone back. I fully expected the officer to deny us a visit. Instead, he hung up and told us to remove our shoes before going through the metal detector.

McIlroy might lecture us when we returned to Waterfall, but if we could glean some information out of Amber, it would be worth it.

Head high, I moseyed through the detector after handing the officer my car keys and driver's license. Shar wasn't so lucky.

"Anything in your pockets?" The officer waved a wand up and down her. The wand beeped at her chest. "Wire in your bra?"

"These babies don't stay up by themselves at my age." Shar hiked her chin.

"You'll have to change to a non-wire. I can't let you proceed otherwise."

"I didn't bring one." She glanced wide-eyed at

me.

"There's a store two miles down the road." The officer planted himself in front of her.

"Excuse me." I stepped around him. "We'll be back." I marched from the prison, across the parking lot, and into my car. "I thought you checked the website for all the rules?" I glared as Shar slid in.

"I stopped reading at the forbidden colors of clothing." She clicked her seat belt into place. "Nowhere did I read anything about a woman's underwear."

"What about food or drink?" I craved a coffee.

"Only on approved days once a month."

I parked in front of the store and climbed out. Maybe they would have coffee in a bottle I could guzzle down before returning to the prison. Inside, I headed one way, Shar the other. Yes. They had a cooler with drinks. I snagged a coffee, then a bag of powdered doughnuts on my way to the register.

Shar huffed as she paid for her purchase. "I have plenty of sports bras at home. I really don't need another one."

"You should have read the rules better."

The cashier laughed. "Women coming in here to buy something without wires keep us in business."

Shar noticed the items in my hand. "I want the same."

Rolling my eyes, I fetched her some. "Come on, time is a'wasting." I set the items on the counter. "You're buying."

"Fine." She shook her head. "Something sure twisted your panties into a wad. All this bother will be worth it when Amber spills her guts. We can warm Amber up by telling her about this morning's adventure."

Our next attempt to visit Amber went through without a hitch. Now, we stood in yet another room until a door unlocked, and we entered what resembled my high school cafeteria.

Round tables with four chairs, vending machines, and a bookcase holding games. A guard sat on a high platform. I told him who we were there to see, then joined Shar at one of the tables.

"You should have brought quarters," she said. "What if we get hungry?"

"Then we'll leave."

"What if Amber doesn't want to see us?"

"Then it'll be a very short stay for us." I kept my gaze on the door at the opposite end of the room.

After what seemed like hours, a sullen-faced Amber entered the room. I almost didn't recognize her without her carefully done hair and makeup. Frowning, she sat across from us.

"What?"

Shar immediately told her about our morning. "Isn't that a hoot?"

Amber blinked like an owl suddenly exposed to bright light. "You came to tell me about your morning?"

"No, we're here to ask you some questions." I shot Shar an exasperated look.

"About what?" Amber crossed her arms. "You're the reason I'm in this place. Why should I tell you anything?"

I almost told her she was in prison because of her own action but held my tongue. "Someone is trying to kill me. I think it has something to do with Jenkins."

"All right. You have my attention."

I went on to tell her about the classifieds, Sarah's murder, and the newspaper articles. "Do you have any idea what is going on?"

She pursed her lips. "Let me think." She drummed her fingers on the table. "I agree it has to do with the attention you brought to yourself."

"Did Jenkins have any family?" Shar asked. "Someone that might have lost a great deal because of his arrest?"

She leaned forward. "I think he has an ex-wife."

That was news. "In Waterfall?"

"No. I don't think she's even in the state. It's something he let slip once when I entered his office without waiting for him to tell me to come in. He'd been on the phone, angry and yelling something about the other person having taken him for all he had and wouldn't get another dime."

"That could be blackmail. Not necessarily an ex."

"Before he noticed me standing there, he muttered something about a she being the worst mistake he'd ever made." She grinned. "He also has a storage unit the cops didn't know about. It's in Blytheville. Number thirteen. I bet you'll find all kinds of interesting things in there."

"Why are you so willing to tell us all this?" Shar tilted her head. "It would seem you'd be holding a grudge."

"Life is boring in here. Besides, Jenkins must have slipped up somewhere or we wouldn't have gotten caught. I told him not to be so sloppy in cutting corners on that theater. Talking to the two of you is the most interesting thing that's happened since my arrest." She stood. "Come again. I'm dying to know what's in that storage unit."

"I'll be sure to let you know." I rattled off my phone number. "I'll put money on the phone so you can call me if you think of anything else."

Amber nodded, then went to stand in front of the door she'd entered through.

Clearly dismissed, Shar and I left. I sat in the driver's seat of my car, deep in thought. I really hadn't expected so much information from Amber. And there was also that trace of disdain for her ex-partner in crime.

"That woman had looser lips than I thought she would." Shar echoed my thoughts. "Feel like visiting a storage unit tonight?"

"Why wait until tonight?" I started the car.

"I think snooping should be done under the cover of darkness. If we're seen by whoever wants you dead, then we might meet an untimely demise." She wiggled her eyebrows.

Sure, she could joke. The target wasn't quite as large on her back.

The drive back passed quicker as we discussed what we'd learned. Since the day wasn't completely gone, I stopped at the pet store and stared at the shattered front window. I quickly cut the engine and bolted from the car.

"Heather!" I stopped in the middle of the room.

"I'm here." She came from the back.

"What happened? Are you okay?" I clutched her shoulders.

"I'm fine. A little shaken up, but I'll survive. Someone left you a message via a rock through the window. I quickly moved the Great Dane puppies into the grooming room. Oh, someone called earlier. They want both of them." She pointed out a sheet of paper on the counter. "It happened just a few minutes ago. McIlroy said he'd send an officer over."

Shar read the note, "Stop snooping or you'll lose that cute little nose, along with other body parts." Her eyes widened. "That's gross and sounds like a child wrote it."

Frightening was more like it. Rather than a child, the writer seemed unhinged. I whirled at the sound of footsteps and stared into the concerned face of McIlroy.

He eyed the shards of glass on the floor. "Anyone hurt?"

"No," Heather said. "I was the only one inside. The note is on the counter."

Keeping a stony face, he read the note, then dropped it and the rock into an evidence bag. "I need you to stop snooping, Miss Ashford. Heed the warning in this note. It's too dangerous. Did you learn anything at the prison?"

Choosing not to tell him about the storage unit until there was something to tell, I said, "Amber seems to be very unhappy with Jenkins. She blamed me at first for sending her to prison, then blamed him. Oh, and she thinks he has an ex-wife somewhere."

He didn't seem surprised at the news.

"You knew?"

Still no expression.

If he was going to keep secrets from me...well, two could play that game. I'd tell him everything...eventually.

"Stay out of my investigation, or face the possibility of arrest."

"A few months ago you asked for my help."

"Not this time." He proceeded to ignore me and took Heather's statement. When he'd finished, he marched from the store without a backward glance.

"He knows something we don't, and whatever it is has him worried," Shar said, retrieving a broom from the supply closet. "Someone should call to have the window boarded."

I left that task to Heather and sagged into my chair behind the counter. Shar was right. McIlroy knew something that had him threatening me with jail time in order to keep me out of things.

Too late for that. I was in this way too deep.

Chapter Thirteen

"Where's Brad?" Shar asked when she arrived at the penthouse and slid into the passenger seat of my car. "And why are you bringing the beast?" She frowned over her shoulder at Sheba.

"Brad has a late meeting, and Sheba is our lookout and warning."

"She's more likely to lick the person to death."

"Hush. Her training is going very well, isn't it, sweetie?" I reached around and patted my dog's head. "Don't listen to the mean lady."

"What do you think we'll find?" Shar asked as we zipped down the interstate toward Blytheville.

"As long as it isn't body parts, I don't care." I shuddered. Bringing Sheba along had another purpose. If there were body parts in the storage unit, she'd find them before one of us did.

"At least you left your bad mood behind." Shar propped her feet on my dashboard. "You were cranky earlier today."

"Because your lack of investigating a website almost made the day a complete waste." Next time, I'd check things out myself.

"So sue me." She grinned. "I guess we're looking for proof Jenkins is/was married, since McIlroy clamped his handsome lips together. Once we find that out, we can determine why they were arguing when Amber overheard him. Someone is upset that he is now behind bars." She waggled her finger at me. "That's why they're after you."

"Yep. Figured that out already." Finding an ex-wife might give us another very important clue, though. I didn't think it was a woman after me, but since I believed in equal rights, I wouldn't discount the idea. "We definitely need another potential suspect to question."

"Oh." She sat up straight. "What if Roberts is now seeing Jenkins' ex? Maybe he's wrapped around her little finger and she has him do her dirty work, which means he palms the job off on someone like that Michael fellow?"

"That's a stretch, even for you." I cut her a sideways glance.

"Yes, but it is plausible. You owe me a day off if I'm right."

Not thinking for a minute she could be right, I said, "If you're right, you can be a traveling groomer."

"It's a deal."

While I agreed with her in regard to Roberts assigning his dirty jobs to someone else, I couldn't imagine him doing the bidding of a woman. He'd always given off a somewhat chauvinistic vibe to me.

The gate to the storage unit was locked up tight. Since I didn't have the code to punch in, we were stuck finding a different way in. I drove past the storage units and parked next to a gas station. We looked like regular customers, except for the bolt cutters Shar grabbed from the backseat.

"Ready?" she whispered.

"There's no need to whisper. No one is paying us any attention." I looped Sheba's leash around my wrist and led the way back to the storage units, eyeing the six-foot iron fence. "I think we can squeeze through." We were sooo trespassing.

I slipped by leg through the bars, shimmied the rest of me after, then helped Sheba in. "Your turn."

Shar stared at her chest. "I don't think I'll fit."

"Smoosh 'em. Hurry up before someone sees us." A homeless man, maybe a drug addict, paused his rambling on the other street of the street and stared our way.

Shar dropped the bolt cutters on my side of the fence and squeezed her lower half through before getting stuck. "Ow! I told you I was too big."

"Clamp them down and wiggle. You only need an inch."

Sheba sat and watched the proceedings with what looked like humor on her doggie face. Occasionally, she'd glance at the man across the street but didn't seem too concerned about him.

Finally, Shar made it through. "That's going to leave bruises."

I laughed and patted her shoulder. "You still

have to go back through when we're finished."

"I'd rather stay in the unit and die."

Using a small flashlight with a big beam, I found number thirteen and held out my hand. "Bolt cutters."

"I want to do it." Shar drew back.

"There isn't a need for both of us to be arrested for breaking and entering."

"Been there, done that. Step aside, sweetie." With one quick snap, the chain holding the unit door fell to the ground with a clatter. "Do you think the cameras work?"

My blood drained to my feet. "What cameras?"

"The ones on every corner."

I glanced around wishing I'd worn my dark hoodie despite the summer heat. We were so busted. "I hope not."

"Sometimes these lower income neighborhoods only put them up for show. Let's focus on that." Shar rolled up the door.

I shined the light over boxes, crates, a vintage bicycle, some garbage bags and...a freezer. "Go, Sheba." I whispered, most definitely letting the dog go in first.

"Let's find something that lets us know without a doubt this is Jenkins' stuff. Then, we'll try to find answers as to why Amber sent us here." I set the flashlight on top of a stack of boxes and closed the rolling door.

Sheba nosed around the freezer but didn't whine or scratch. Maybe it really was empty or simply held more boxes. Some of the tension in my shoulders relaxed, and I turned to the first box.

A coat of dust covered everything, and I sneezed as I opened the flap. "Doesn't look as if anyone has been here in a long time."

"This old bike is a woman's. Do you think anyone would mind if I took it?" Shar ran her hand over the banana seat.

"That would be stealing, and you'd never squeeze it through the fence."

"Why would Jenkins have a woman's bike?"

"Sentimental reasons?" I shrugged and dug through a pile of vintage pinup-girl magazines. Those would bring a pretty penny if sold at an auction. The next box contained cloisonné vases and candlesticks. I stopped digging and stepped back.

Everything held objects of monetary value. If Jenkins stashed these things away, why cut corners on the buildings he constructed? I broached the subject with Shar.

"Maybe all these things belong to his wife, and he doesn't want her to have them out of spite." She opened the freezer. "Lots of freezer bags in here." She pulled one out and tossed it to me.

I jumped back. "I'm not opening it."

"I don't want to. Besides, it can't be part of a body. The freezer isn't plugged in. It would stink to high heaven in here."

True. I bent and picked up the bag, peered inside, and gasped. "It's full of money."

Shar leaned against the freezer. "It doesn't make sense. Jenkins isn't dead. He could tell someone this is all here. So why target you? You sent him to jail; you didn't cut out his tongue. We're missing something…like the reason someone hates you."

"Stop bringing that up." Chills spiraled through me every time I heard the words. "Keep looking for clues."

Sheba started sniffing at the door, then froze, staring as something shuffled on the other side. A tenant? Or someone here to stop us. Without the lock, we froze. When no more sounds came, we turned back to the task at hand.

In a plastic crate with a lid, I found tax documents all in the name of Harold and Margaret Jenkins dated two years ago. "Bingo." I felt pretty certain that these documents would show something illegal. "We need to find his wife."

Shar clapped. "I'm going to be a traveling groomer."

"That isn't for sure." I frowned. Although I was starting to think the ex might be involved up to her neck.

Sheba growled.

I put a finger to my lips and clicked off the flashlight, plunging us into total darkness. When no one opened the door, I turned the light back on. "Definitely time to get out of here. I'm taking the tax returns."

"What about the money?"

"We'll tell McIlroy about it when we hand over these files." I slowly opened the door, cringing at the screech of metal wheels in need of oiling. Funny I hadn't noticed the sound until now.

I glanced both ways and waved Shar forward. Once she slipped out, I lowered the door and made a dash for the fence. "I'll go through first, then you'll have to hand me the crate over the top. I'll catch it."

"You're too short."

"No, I'm not." Yes, I was. I slipped through and glanced around for something to stand on. A couple of cement blocks nestled in tall weeds. "Hold on." I stacked the blocks and stepped up. "Hand it over."

"You ladies need any help?"

Sheba growled.

I whirled, falling off my platform. "No, thank you."

The man I'd seen across the street earlier, grinned, missing some teeth. "Mighty suspicious to see two ladies breaking into a storage unit."

Sheba stepped between me and the man.

He took a step back. "I can take a hint. If you give me twenty dollars, I'll keep my mouth shut."

"For crying out loud. That's bribery." Shar fished a twenty from the pocket of her pants and held it through the bars. "Now, go away."

He gave a sarcastic salute, a wary glance at Sheba, and strolled toward the gas station whistling.

"Hurry, Shar. We're attracting too much attention." I stepped back up and accepted the crate she half handed, half tossed to me.

"Here goes the torture." She sucked in her gut and squeezed in, getting very stuck.

"Sucking in your stomach made your chest bigger. Exhale."

"I'm trying." She groaned, rolling her shoulders forward. "Uh oh." She glanced behind me.

I whirled to see a very amused McIlroy standing there. "Don't just stand there, help her."

"This is far more entertaining."

"How'd you find us?" Shar asked.

"Cameras."

"Oh. They do work. Any suggestions for getting me out of here?"

"I could call the fire department—"

"No!" She was on the verge of tears. "I'd never survive the shame."

"You got yourself in, you should be able to get yourself out." He turned to me. "Whatever that is, hand it over."

"Tax documents on Jenkins and his wife. Number thirteen is full of cash and antiques. We cut the lock, so you might want to get a new one put on before someone takes everything." I handed him the crate.

"I need ice." Shar stepped next to me. "I'll have bruises upon bruises."

McIlroy's lips twitched, then he grew serious again. "Why don't the two of you apply for private investigator licenses and spare me the decision of whether to arrest you or not?"

"It's too much fun making your blood pressure rise," Shar said. "Although I can think of better ways which are a lot more fun."

He cleared his throat. "Go home. I'll take things from here."

I released the breath I'd been holding. We weren't going to be arrested after all.

In the car, Shar sighed and leaned her head against the back of the seat. "I left the bolt cutters in the unit. Plus, we got away with nothing."

"Not necessarily." I smiled, pulling back onto

the road. "I memorized the last address of one Margaret Jenkins as of her last joint tax return. That might lead to where she's currently residing."

Shar held up her hand for a high-five. "Plus, tomorrow is Ladies Night at the Club. We can ask Lucy if she knows where the ex-wife lives. If she does, it saves us a step."

I returned the high-five. Our investigation was moving forward quite nicely. We weren't attacked or arrested. I could only pray my luck continued.

Chapter Fourteen

"Good morning." Brad handed me a coffee the next morning, then kissed me. "Sorry I got home so late. You were already asleep with the door closed when I returned."

"What time did you come home?"

"About midnight."

"I don't think I was home yet." I filled him in on last night's details, even Shar getting stuck in the fence.

He went from disbelief, to amusement, to relief in the space of my talking. "I wish you would have waited for me. We could have gone tonight."

"Tonight, Shar and I are going to the club to talk to Lucy." I spit out the word, club. The desperation of the beautiful women who wanted to land sugar daddies, the pettiness, the sadness. Until a few months ago, I hadn't known anything about the mistresses of many of our town's wealthy men. As far as I was concerned, Women's Night was only worth whatever information I could glean in regard to whatever mystery I was trying to solve.

"Besides, we have to act as soon as we know about something," I said. "Otherwise, the evidence could be gone."

"Well, I can't go with you to the club, obviously. Please be careful. Do you mind if I put a tracking app on your phone? As much as I'd like to lock you in the penthouse, I know I can't. This way at least, I know where you are if something happens."

What a sweetheart to ask permission. My independence had finally sunk in, and for that I gave my permission and handed him my phone. "Only if I can also track you."

"Not a problem." He grinned. "This will pinpoint the phone's location up to twenty feet. How about I take you to dinner one night this week? It's been a while since we've gone out."

"What? You're bored of popcorn and a movie on the sofa?" I arched a brow. "Not that we've been able to do much of that lately. Yes, I'd love to." We desperately needed some one-on-one time together.

"Great. I'll see you tonight." Another sweet kiss, and he left.

"Why don't you head to the thrift store?" Shar said, entering the front room. "See if you can find a new dress. You don't want to wear the same one you wore the last time."

"Why not? It's been several months."

"Oh, they'll remember, mark my words. They'll remember and compare. Don't forget. You're the woman on Brad's arm. They would all jump to take your place."

I rolled my eyes. Thankfully, Brad wasn't interested in overly made-up gold diggers. I grabbed my purse. "I'll be back in a bit." I hated shopping but could always wear the dress when Brad took me out to dinner. Shar was right. Since I dated the state's most eligible bachelor, I should at least look the part.

I opened the door, shot out my leg to keep Moses from slipping past me, and quickly stepped outside with a wag of my finger at the cat. "Keep trying to escape and I'll keep you at the penthouse, you naughty boy." My two felines watched the proceedings from their perch on the counter, no doubt watching and learning so they could plot their own escape. My eyes narrowed at them.

Trashcan groomed himself, ignoring my threat. Sharkbait simply turned his back so he couldn't see me.

I chuckled and marched toward Someone Else's Junk. A bell jingled over the door as I entered.

Mrs. Murdock, the proprietor, popped up from behind the counter like a child's toy. "Trinity, it's been a while."

"I'm in need of a new cocktail dress."

"Oh, goodie. I love helping you dress up." She bustled to the back of the store. "I've had several donated since prom is over. I'm sure we can find you something spectacular." She flipped through the dresses on the rack. "Heard you found Sarah's body."

"My dog did." I sighed.

"Sarah shopped here quite a bit. Never donated anything, but well, everyone knows the woman couldn't get rid of anything. I've heard she owns a regular house, not just the manufactured one, and it's full to the ceiling."

Interesting. "Do you know where it is?"

"Of course, I do. We were friends. It's out on Old Mill Road. Been there a long time. Mostly covered by trees and brush now. She pretty much left it alone once it was filled up. You think there might be a clue in there?"

"Maybe. Let me see that maroon-colored dress, please."

She handed me a dress with a tight-fitting bodice and a skirt that flared from the waist to flutter around my knees. Adorable. I couldn't wait to try it on.

Inside the dressing room, I quickly donned the dress and immediately felt pretty. "I'll take it," I called through the curtain. "It's perfect." I glanced at the price tag. Fifty dollars didn't bother me as much as it once did. My little pet store/daycare was doing quite well, thank you.

"I had it dry cleaned before hanging it on the rack, so you're good to go."

"Perfect." I handed her the dress and followed her to the register. "Does anyone know about Sarah's house?"

Mrs. Murdoch shook her head. "She was too embarrassed about her…addiction, she called it. The house once belonged to a cousin. Sarah never put her name on the title."

News McIlroy wouldn't likely have. "Thank

you." I took my purchase and returned to the store to find a man finishing the installation of a new front window. "This is fast."

"Requests of Mr. Armstrong. He pulled me from the theater job to do this." The man glared at me. "Guess it pays to be the boss man's harlot."

"Excuse me?" My face had to be as red as the evening sun because my blood reached boiling level. "What's your name?"

"Lance Jenkins." He leered once more, then marched toward a waiting truck.

Mouth open, I watched him squeal tires from the parking lot. We might have found our missing link. I put my new dress in my car and called Brad.

"He said what?" His voice had a growl.

"If this is how people think of me, I don't want to stay in the penthouse anymore."

"You're in the guest room, Trinity. Ignore him. He's obviously sore with you."

"Do you think he's related to Harold?"

"I have a strong suspicion after this. I didn't hire the guy. He's part of the crew that came with the new construction company. I'll be letting his boss know about today's behavior, that's for sure."

I leaned against my car and blinked away tears. Now that my anger had ebbed, I wanted to cry tears of shame. No one had ever called me a bad name before, especially one I didn't deserve.

"Forget it, sweetheart. Don't let the words of a bad person ruin your day."

"You're right." I didn't want to lose the joy I'd received over buying a new-to-me dress. "See you tonight." I hung up, lifted my chin, and marched inside the store.

~

"That dress is a stunner," Shar said when I came down the stairs.

Brad had taken the animals home with him, and I'd changed in my apartment upstairs, not wanting him to see me in the dress until our dinner date. I twirled. "Makes me feel like a princess."

"Oh, to be young again." Shar had toned down her bling this time. Instead of multi-colored sequins on a jacket, she'd chosen a royal blue dress covered with sequins.

"You look very nice, too."

"We should do something wrong so McIlroy can get an eyeful of me in this dress. That man is so very difficult to stand up and take notice when a woman is coming on to him."

"Then why go after him?" I asked, following her to the Thunderbird.

"Look at him. I'd be a fool not to try."

He was handsome for a fifty-year-old. I slid into the passenger seat. As she drove, I told her about the window installer.

She braked, whipping my head back and forth and causing several vehicles to lay on their horns as they swerved around us. "Harold has a son?"

"Maybe." I shrugged. "It's definitely worth looking into." I then told her about Sarah's filled-up house.

"Looks like we have a few paths to follow in the next few days."

"I'll find out from Brad the name of the construction company and pay them a visit. The house will have to wait. I don't relish going into the woods, to a house I'm assuming has no electricity and might be a hazard in the dark."

"I should buy some spotlights if we're going to make a habit of this investigative stuff."

"Don't be crazy. I have no intention of making this a habit."

We pulled up to the country club, and Shar handed the valet the car keys. "Not a scratch, my boy, or it will be your head."

"Yes, ma'am." He stared at the car in awe. "I'll care for it like a baby."

Shar nodded, then headed for the club entrance, head high. I followed, albeit reluctantly.

Once inside, I snatched a flute of champagne from a passing waiter so I'd have something to do with my hands and stepped onto the patio where the women gathered. I'd gotten used to the stares. Shar was right. Any one of them would take my place in a heartbeat.

Before remembering Summer had gone back to Oklahoma, I scanned the crowd for her. We'd managed to become friends of sorts. I was happy she'd gone back to her upbringing. Shar and I parted ways in order to cover more ground.

"Look who's feeling better." Lucy glided to her feet from a cushioned chair. "Heard you kissed a tree."

"Word gets around." I peered at her over the rim of my glass.

"It sure does. Did you enjoy your visit with Amber?" She smiled, tilting her head.

"How would you know about that?"

"Unfortunately, Joe allows her to call him, even after she embarrassed him by trying to kill your man."

"That's nice of him."

"Niceness has nothing to do with why. He's afraid she'll spill all his secrets." Her eyes glittered. "I know why you're here, Trinity. Same reason you sought me out at the gym. You want to know whether I know anything that will help you find Sarah's killer. Well, I don't. You might want to speak with Amelia Turner. Roberts and Jenkins go way back." Still smiling, she turned and headed to speak with someone I didn't know.

I ran my gaze over the others in search of Amelia. There. Shar had her cornered near the fountain. Pasting a smile on my face, I headed their way.

"There is no way in Hades I'll tell you anything." Amelia glared. "You know what happens to snitches."

"Yeah, yeah, they get stitches. Don't be a baby." Shar crossed her arms. "It's only a matter of time before he's behind bars, and you have to find another man to support you. Rich men are rare around these parts. We know he sells stolen cars. We know he hires people to do his dirty work. We just need proof."

"Get it somewhere else." She spun and stormed away.

"That wasn't a pleasant conversation," I said.

"No. Did you have any luck?"

"Lucy told me to talk to Amelia."

"Dead end. Now, who here might have loose

lips?" She turned in a slow circle, then grinned. "Why haven't we ever thought to speak with one of the servers?" She motioned to where a waitress slipped into the women's restroom.

"No idea." I set my almost full flute of champagne on a table and followed the server.

"I can't, Michael," She spoke on the phone in one of the stalls. "If anyone finds out you're staying at my house, I'll go to jail for harboring a fugitive."

I exchanged an excited glance with Shar, then knocked on the stall door.

"Busy!"

"I think you need to come out," I said, stepping back.

"I'll call you back." The woman joined us. "What?"

"Tell us how you know Michael Watson."

"Why should I tell you anything?"

"Because he ran me off the road and almost killed me. I'd like to speak with him about why."

"You'll tell the cops."

"Maybe, maybe not. Depends on what information he's willing to spill."

Chapter Fifteen

"How do you know Michael?" I repeated. "What's your name?"

"Shelby Hanover. Michael is…was my foster brother." She chewed the cuticle on her thumb, clearly perplexed as to how to proceed. "I knew he was mixed up in something, but I didn't think he'd try to kill someone."

"Well, he did, and we—" I wiggled my finger between myself and Shar, "strongly believe he buried a murdered woman."

Her eyes widened, and she gasped. "Not Michael!"

"Yep. So, will you take us to him now?"

"I'll have to call a ride."

"We'll take you." Shar gripped her arm. "Wouldn't want you alerting your brother, now would we?"

Like a beaten puppy, Shelby let herself be

led/dragged past many curious faces to the Thunderbird. I let her sit up front, taking a seat in the back in order to keep an eye on her.

"What was Michael asking you to do for him?" I tapped her on the shoulder.

"Go to his apartment and retrieve some things. If he did something as horrible as you say he did, the cops will be watching his place."

"Yeah, I'm not buying that. You said you knew he was mixed up in something but not murder. What do you think he's into?"

"Fine. Drugs, okay? I don't want to retrieve drugs from his place and get caught with them. So sue me." She crossed her arms and huffed.

"No worries there." Shar glanced at me in the rearview mirror. "We're great at getting in and out of places. Grabbing those drugs will give us some bargaining power."

As crazy as the idea was, I agreed. Michael would be more willing to talk to us if we had something he wanted. "Show us the way, Shelby."

"Y'all are going to get me killed."

Undeterred by her tearful response, Shar pressed for directions. We pulled in front of a shoddy duplex on the outskirts of town. "Do you have a key, or do we have to break in?" Shar asked.

"I have a key." Shelby glanced around. "I don't see anyone, do you? We have to be careful."

The girl's fear started to rub off on me. I stared out each window. "Looks clear to me. Let's make this quick. Shar, keep the car running." I shoved open my door at the same time as Shelby. We sprinted for the front door.

After a bit of a fumble inserting the key, she opened the door, slamming it closed behind us. "They're in a backpack in his bedroom."

"Lead the way." I stopped her from turning on a light. "Let your eyes adjust. We don't want anyone suspicious about a light being on at midnight."

"Smart. Are y'all crooks?"

"Straddling the line. Let's move." I gave her a little shove.

By now, we could see well enough and hurried down a short hallway to the last room on the right. I felt safe enough to turn on the light inside the walk-in closet. An army green backpack had been shoved behind a laundry hamper. I grabbed the handle. "This one?" I unzipped it to see bags of white powder and marijuana. "Yep."

Shelby's phone rang.

"Don't answer that." I put my hand on her arm. "Do not warn Michael. I'm serious. If you do, I'll let my detective friend know all about this and you." I held up the pack.

"Okay." After making sure the coast outside was clear, we made a dash for the Thunderbird. Seconds later, Shar sped toward our next destination.

Shelby's apartment was in a unit of twelve, two buildings with three apartments on top and three on the bottom. A bit better than Michael's but not by much. "I'm upstairs, the last one," she said. "We don't have to worry so much about being watched. These folks are cool and not druggies."

Until Michael moved in, anyway. Shar and I followed her upstairs, me still clutching the backpack. I had no plans on releasing it to anyone but McIlroy. But first, I needed some information from Michael.

"Michael?" Shelby pushed open her door. "Now, don't get mad."

Shar and I entered to see a startled Michael sitting on a worn leather sofa, beer in hand. He bolted to his feet. "Do you know what you've done?" He glared at Shelby.

"Sit down and shut up," Shar said. "We forced her to bring us. As you'll learn soon enough, we can be very persuasive." She pulled a Taser from her clutch.

"Put that away," I hissed.

"Nope. Not until we get what we came for." A menacing look came over her features.

The young man's gaze landed on the backpack in my hand. "Oh, no, Shelby. You're going to get us killed."

"Like you tried to kill me?" I arched a brow. "I know you work for Roberts stealing cars and helping him resell them. Am I right? Did you murder Sarah Turner?"

"No!"

"But you buried her body, right?"

He nodded, falling back onto the sofa, splashing beer from the can onto his shirt. "Please, don't ask me questions."

"Too bad. That's what we're here for. Sit down, Shelby." I glared at the woman inching her way toward the door. "Tell me, who killed Sarah?"

"I don't know. I'm available for hire."

"What does that mean?"

"It means someone calls me, gives me a job to do, I do it, then I get paid." He took a swig from the can. "I got a call to bury a body dumped at the lake. Got paid five-hundred dollars to bury her. Not bad for a couple hour's work."

"Oh, Michael." Shelby covered her face with her hands and sobbed.

I couldn't allow her heartache to prevent me from moving forward with interrogating the man. "Who are you dealing for?"

"Please, stop questioning me."

"If you want these," I held up the pack, "you'll answer my questions."

"Have you heard Roberts has a rival?"

I nodded. "Go on."

"The new guy is Orlando Jones out of Little Rock. He ventures further than Roberts does and dabbles in more than stolen cars. I figured Waterfall was a good place for me to be the number one dealer, so I approached him with my plan. He isn't going to be happy about this."

"Boo-hoo," Shar said. "There's always consequences to any action."

"Where can we find Jones?"

"You don't want to."

"Is he here in Waterfall or still in Little Rock?"

"Blytheville. He's a big corporate man. I've never met him in person. Can I have my stuff now?"

"Well—" I jumped back as the door slammed open and McIlroy and Rickson entered, guns drawn.

"Hands up," McIlroy ordered.

I dropped the backpack like it had suddenly

gotten very hot and put my hands up.

Shar dropped the Taser. "What's going on?"

"Looks like a drug drop to me," he said.

"How'd you know we were here?" She narrowed her eyes.

"Neighbors said they saw a couple of prostitutes enter this apartment with a backpack. We put two and two together. Rickson, take these women outside. I'll take care of the bag and the other two."

What in the world was going on? The detective treated us like criminals.

"How dare you call us prostitutes!" Shar aimed a kick at his leg, drawing back at the last minutes. "I don't want to add assaulting an officer to my list of alleged crimes." Nose in the air, she stepped out of the apartment, me on her heels.

"Are you arresting us?" Shar asked. "Because I'm not leaving my baby here."

His eyes widened. "Where is the baby?"

"My car." She rolled her eyes.

"I don't know." He opened the backdoor to the squad car. "I was told to put you in here. Just following orders."

Another squad car pulled up. Minutes later, Shelby and Michael were in the backseat of their car.

McIlroy put the backpack in the trunk of the car we were in, then opened the back door. "Keys." He held out his hand. "Unless you want your car stolen."

Shar pulled the keys from her clutch. "Can I have my Taser back?"

"At the station." He slammed the door and

marched to the Thunderbird.

Rickson slid into the driver's seat. "Does that answer your question?"

"Yeah." McIlroy was making good on his threat of arresting us. I knew Brad would post bail, but it still sliced at my heart that I'd have to ask him. That's what I received for trying to help the authorities.

"Chin up, buttercup. Getting arrested only makes us more interesting." Shar grinned. "It's not so bad."

"You've got a rap sheet?"

"Nah." She shrugged. "Well, protests mainly. Those don't really count."

I smirked. If a person is booked, it counts.

At the station, Rickson put the two of us in an interrogation room, fetched us each a glass of water, then left us alone.

"I'm still upset that someone called us prostitutes," Shar said. "We look classy."

"All someone saw was two dressed-up women enter an apartment at midnight with a third younger woman."

It didn't take long for McIlroy to join us. He sat across from us and exhaled heavily. "You two are going to be the death of me."

"How did you find us?" I asked.

"The tracker on your phone. Brad got worried because you weren't home and weren't headed in the right direction. So, I went looking for you and overheard you interrogating Michael Watson." He rubbed both hands down his face. "Seriously. Get a license and do this legally. The two of you have balls of steel."

"And brains." Shar tapped her forefinger against her temple. "I'm relieved that no one thought us prostitutes."

"Would you stop worrying about that?" I shot her a glare before returning my attention to the detective. "So, you aren't arresting us?"

"I probably should, but no. We made a pretense of doing so in hopes of saving your lives. Jones is not someone to mess with."

"You know who he is?"

He nodded. "Came from California last year and set up shop. We've been trying to get evidence on him ever since. Your little adventure tonight has helped. He cannot find out you willingly gave me anything, understand?"

"Absolutely." I stood. "Can we go home now?"

"Yes." He tossed Shar her keys. "Try to stay out of trouble for a few days, all right? Let me breathe a little."

"It's sweet how worried you are about us." Shar blew him a kiss and sashayed out the door.

"Just ask her to dinner, why don't you?" I smiled. "She's driving me crazy."

He gave a rare grin. "She does the same to me, but I'm pretty sure I can't handle a woman like her. Go home and relieve Brad's mind. Good job tonight, by the way."

"Thanks." I hurried outside.

Shar dropped me off in front of the building that housed the penthouse, and I practically ran to the elevator. Two minutes later, I was in Brad's arms, being thoroughly kissed and returning the action equally.

Once we were breathless, I kicked off my heels and plopped on the sofa to tell him all about our evening.

"So, Roberts and Jenkins are friends. Amber still calls Roberts. There's a new dealer in town. Sarah has a house full of junk that you and Shar are going to visit."

"That sums it up." I nestled against him. "I should really go to bed."

"Why visit Sarah's house? Do you really think she kept something that will point to her killer?"

"Possibly." I reluctantly pulled away. "I'm beat. See you in the morning." I gave him a tender kiss before heading to my room. Despite my exhaustion, I lay in bed and stared at the ceiling. I was thankful for the tracker on my phone. Hopefully, it had provided Shar and myself with a cover by letting McIlroy know our whereabouts.

If the ruse didn't work, I could very well have a gangster boss after me. That was a first.

Chapter Sixteen

"We're out of pets," Heather said the instant she walked in the door of Tail Waggin'.

"What?" I stared at my two cats taking over my desk behind the counter. Since I hadn't had my coffee yet, my brain wasn't fully awake yet.

"Pets. To Sell." She slowed her speech and stored her purse in the drawer under the counter we kept locked during the day. "It was a great idea, Trinity. How was your night?"

"Girl, let me tell you." Shar slapped the counter. "What a hoot! We were almost arrested for being prostitutes, in theory."

I rolled my eyes and told the real story. "It was all for our protection."

Heather leaned her elbows on the table and rested her chin in her hands. "Y'all live an exciting life."

"Don't worry." Shar patted her on the shoulder.

"When that deadbeat dad of Robbie's gets out of prison, he'll have visitation rights, and you can join us on our adventures."

"I'd rather live vicariously through the two of you. I'll still have a child to take care of." She smiled and went to open the door for Brad whose hands were full with coffee cups.

"How are the three most beautiful women in Waterfall?" He handed us each our favorite brew. When the other two left to start their work, Brad leaned across the counter and kissed me. "I have to leave town for a few days. Promise me you'll take advantage of all the security available at the penthouse."

"I promise." Maybe I was starting to enjoy having a man look after to me…in a fashion. "I'll miss you. When do you leave?"

"Now. I've got to meet with Dad's lawyer to finalize things. Be safe, sweetheart." He gave a crooked grin. "McIlroy has promised to keep an eye on you."

"Oh, goodie."

He laughed. "He won't be too heavy-handed." He gave me another kiss, this one more lingering. "I'll miss you, too."

My throat clogged as he marched out the door. We hadn't been apart much since the mystery surrounding Jenkins. I wasn't sure how I could face the large penthouse without him. Thank goodness for the four fur babies who would be there with me.

The bell over the door jingled. I glanced up to see an elderly woman pulling a little red wagon into the store. "Welcome. May I help you?"

"I'm helping you, dear." She reached into the wagon and lifted out a tiny Dachshund puppy. "I have five. Will you sell them for me?"

"It will be my pleasure." I snuggled the puppy against my neck, inhaling its puppy breath. "These little beauties will sell fast."

"I hope so. I can really use the money."

I studied her tattered coat and the faded wagon. "How about I buy them from you right now?" I reached for the business checkbook. "Then, you're free to do what you need to."

Tears sprang to her eyes as she clasped her hands under her chin. "That would be a blessing."

I wrote the check knowing I reduced my profit but took pleasure in the fact I could help someone in need. Grinning, I handed her the check.

"You must be the sweetest girl to walk the streets of this town," Shar said once the woman left.

"Far from it, but it did feel good." I got up and put the puppies in the playpen before taking photos and posting them online.

The rest of the day passed with grooming appointments, boarding reservations, and an hour spent spraying empty cages for new occupants. A busy day but a productive one. I could go to Old Mill Road with Shar and not worry that I left work unfinished.

After we closed the store for the day, I took the cats and Sheba to the penthouse, fed them, freshened their water, and then took Sheba back to my car to pick up Shar. While I loved riding in the Thunderbird, I knew she didn't like my fast-growing mastiff in her car.

Sheba's behavior has improved immensely with her training, but she had a ways to go. We all needed to wait it out. My beautiful girl wasn't going anywhere.

"You're late," Shar said sliding into the car. "I'd rather not be in the woods in the dark."

"I had to feed the animals."

"That's why I don't have pets. They take up time. I love working with them but am very happy to send them home. Kind of like a grandmother, I guess."

"Why didn't you ever have any children?"

"I couldn't." She shrugged. "It's okay. My life is good. I have nieces and nephews, so I had my baby fixes." Shar pulled up a map app on her phone. "This house isn't going to be easy to find."

"How many falling-down houses full of junk can there be on Old Mill Road?"

Several, it seemed. Most houses looked vacant as nature took over. "There." I could barely make out the name Turner on one of the rusted mailboxes.

"Good eye. Oh." She squealed as we hit a large pothole.

I slowed our speed and did my best to swerve around the worst of them, stopping in front of a house with a sagging roof that made me catch my breath.

The windows, many broken, showed a hoarder's paradise behind them. It looked as if the stuff inside pushed against the roof, the only thing keeping it from falling in completely. "Are we sure we want to go in there?"

"Nothing is falling unless we move something."

She chuckled. "Let's be careful what we touch. Think of it as a giant game of Jenga."

"Let me drive around back in case anyone drives by. We don't want to be seen."

"Way out here?"

I parked in the back and opened the back passenger door for Sheba. "Come on, girl." Dogs could sense danger, right? "You let us know if the roof is about to fall." With trepidation, I inched toward the front door. Not wanting to risk my dog's safety, I commanded her to stay outside. "You're our watchdog, okay?"

Her tail thumped the ground, stirring up dust.

"Come on." Shar shoved the door open. "Pretty full in here, but there's a path of sorts through the stuff." She squeezed in, leaving me to follow.

Thankfully, the only strong smells greeting us were mold and mildew. I couldn't detect any scent of living or dead.

Towers of boxes filled the front room, the weight crushing the boxes nearer the floor. Papers, clothes, and household goods spilled into the meager path Shar had mentioned. I didn't know where to start looking, especially since we weren't sure what we were looking for.

I had to admit to being fearful of digging through anything. If one of the towers toppled, we'd be crushed, but at least I had a tracker on my phone. Small consolation if I was dead.

Trying to detect a place to start digging, I made my way to the back of the house to what I thought was either once a bedroom or home office. If I had records to keep, they were usually stored in one of those two rooms.

"I'll start in here," Shar said. "Be careful. Move one box at a time and start a new pile where there isn't one. Whatever you do, don't make any of the piles bigger."

No worries there. I'd be moving in slow motion. Taking another wary glance at the cardboard towers around me, I began my search, taking down a box, rifling through it, setting it down, and on and on until I thought I'd drop dead from exhaustion.

"Anything?" Shar called from the other room.

"Not yet. Don't yell too loud or you'll cause an avalanche." I swiped my arm across my perspiring forehead and searched for a place I could take a rest. There were enough boxes from here to there to reveal a dust-covered desk shoved in the corner next to a chair with more duct tape than vinyl.

I climbed over a small mound of miscellaneous objects and fell into the chair wishing I'd brought a bottle of water with me. The dust on everything had me drier than the Sahara. What to do next? What did we actually know about Sarah's murder?

One. She'd had a fascination with newspapers, kept all the articles on me, and something about that act had gotten her killed.

Two. It linked up somehow to Roberts Automotive as evidenced in Sarah's photos.

Three. It also linked up to Howard Jenkins.

Four. I was pretty sure the killer had attended the groundbreaking ceremony of the theater.

Five. Lance Jenkins, a man I'd only met once, seemed to strongly dislike me.

Six. Harold Jenkins was most likely still

married.

Seven…Even with Michael behind bars, someone wanted me dead.

So, I had a lot of assumptions and no concrete proof. I started opening the desk drawers. Nothing…wait a minute. I lifted a false bottom from the top right drawer and pulled out a bright yellow folder. Inside was a much clearer photo of Roberts, but the really interesting thing was the notes Sarah had written about a certain Lance Jenkins with a rap sheet as long as my arm.

How did McIlroy not know about this man? Maybe he did and wasn't sharing. Did the detective know Lance had spoken with me while installing my front window? There were always more questions.

"Gotta go." Shar darted past the room I'd worked in. "Call your dog. A car is coming."

"Sheba!" I grabbed the folder and raced after Shar. Behind me came the padding of Sheba's feet. Good girl. She caught up with us quickly despite the hoard around us.

We toppled boxes away from a broken-out window. It took both of us to lift Sheba up and out, before we climbed to the ground. I grabbed the dog's leash and sprinted for the car.

"How are we getting away without whoever drove up seeing us?" Shar asked.

"I don't know. I guess we wait and make a run for it whenever it's possible. Maybe they won't notice us back here." I turned the key in the ignition in preparation.

I glanced up, my mouth falling open. "Oh, no."

A burning torch flew through the air and landed on the roof. From the growing orange glow, I suspected the front of the house was already ablaze. If Shar hadn't heard the approaching vehicle, we'd be stuck in a death trap.

Shar glanced wide-eyed at me. "What if they come around back?"

"Let's hope they think the job was done. That house is going to burn fast."

Sheba whimpered and cowered in the backseat. I agreed. We really needed to get out of here before any surrounding trees caught fire. "I'm making a run for it. Hold on."

I pressed the gas and careened around the corner of the house as the taillights of a truck disappeared down the road. "Call 911. Report the fire. I'm going to follow the arsonist." Thank goodness, I'd brought the folder with me. "Tomorrow, let's pay a visit to Mrs. Jenkins."

"What did you find?"

"What I think is proof that Harold's son is right in the middle of all this." The Bluetooth in the car alerted me to a text from Heather. "Go ahead and push the button on the screen, Shar. It might be important. She doesn't usually contact me this late."

Shar pressed the button and the electronic voice started reciting the text. "Bobby called. Michael Watson killed on the yard. Prison on lockdown."

"Things are getting real," Shar said, pressing 911 on her phone.

"As if they weren't already." I sped after the truck, hoping to get close enough to catch a glimpse of the license plate.

THE DOG WHO FOUND A BODY

Chapter Seventeen

McIlroy waited on the sidewalk when I arrived the next morning. "Heard you reported a fire last night."

"Come in and I'll tell you all about it. You might want this." I set down the pet crates with the cats, then handed him the folder tucked under my arm since I'd already made copies of everything inside. "Mind telling me about Lance Jenkins?"

"How do you know about him?" McIlroy followed me inside.

"He called me a harlot when he installed my new front window."

"Hold on." His hand shot out and gripped my arm. "You need to tell me more than that."

"So you do know about him." I crossed my arms.

"Of course, I do. I'm not an idiot." He shook his head. "This is bad. You and Shar need to go away for a while."

"I own a business. There are animals depending on me. You've heard about Michael Watson's death, I assume?"

He nodded. "We're putting the pressure on Roberts and trying to locate Lance Jenkins. Nothing concrete so far."

"Have you questioned his mother?" I tilted my head.

"She refuses to speak to me without a warrant. So far, I don't have enough evidence."

"Her son being a suspect in a murder case isn't enough?" I marched around the counter and took a seat.

"The evidence is about her son. We can't find him and have no proof he was anywhere around when Sarah was murdered."

I'd find him that proof. I was also about seventy-five-percent sure that Margaret Jenkins would speak to me. Some people didn't like law enforcement but would spill their guts to the average person, especially if that person was a woman.

"Howdy, handsome." Shar sailed into the room, smiled, and continued to the back.

The detective looked as surprised as I was that she didn't linger to flirt. "Okay, I'll go over what's in this folder. Stay out of trouble, Miss Ashford. I promised Brad you'd still be alive when he returned."

"I'm pretty sure you can call me by my first name by now." But I made no promises. I needed to see this thing through.

"Why do you bring all the animals with you every day?" He glanced at Sheba who sat by his side, big dark eyes trained on him.

"I don't leave them at home alone. Besides, Sheba knows it was Michael Watson who buried Sarah's body. She identified him by the dirt on his shoes."

"Here we go again." He exhaled sharply through his nose. "Animals do not solve crimes."

"Police dogs do."

"No, they only help. Humans solve crimes."

I hitched my chin. "Moses helped bring down Jenkins."

"By creating a distraction."

"The cat identified him by his cologne, same as Sheba did with dirt." I refused to be swayed. My animals were brilliant mystery solvers.

"There's no talking sense to you. I just hope this half-grown dog can help you if the killer gets close." He whirled and stormed from the store.

"What's put a burr under his saddle?" Shar asked, joining me in the front.

"He's unconvinced about the talents of my pets in catching criminals."

"All I can say is I wish Sheba would hurry up and discover who killed Sarah." She turned as Heather entered. "How is your husband?"

"In solitary confinement for his own safety." She plopped her purse on the counter. "He told me the same time he called about Michael. Someone shanked the poor guy as they moved from the cafeteria to their unit."

"He knew something, and someone thought he'd told someone he shouldn't." Shar leaned on the counter. "Wish he would have told us something."

"There is a very important thing he told us," I said, springing up to feed the new puppies for sale. "Orlando Jones."

"Right. Our next interrogation after Margaret Jenkins."

Heather stared from Shar to me. "Don't the two of you ever sleep?"

"Not lately." I scooped food into a dish, then put the puppies in the pen. The best way to sell cute little puppies was to allow someone to hold them.

"What's today's grand adventure?" Heather locked her purse away.

"We plan on visiting Margaret Jenkins. She lives on

the hill in Oakland." A ritzy community about half an hour's drive from Waterfall. I didn't know if she liked animals or not, but I'd be bringing Sheba with us. Despite McIlroy's reservations, I knew in my heart my dog would do everything in her power to protect me from harm.

"I'll be going home, eating macaroni and cheese again, and watching a Disney movie. My life is so mundane."

"Wait until your son becomes a teenager," Shar said. "You'll want to go back to those mundane days when he stays out too late or gets brought home by the cops for underage drinking."

Heather narrowed her eyes. "Excuse me?"

"Happened to my nephew. Could happen to your boy." Shar turned to greet the day's first grooming appointment.

"Don't mind her," I said as Shar carried the poodle to the back. "She doesn't have a filter. Are you all right?"

"No." Tears sprang to her eyes. "I filed for divorce."

"Oh. Well, the papers aren't signed yet. If you're having second—"

"I'm not. I can't live the life Bobby wants. I can't trust him not to put us further in debt with his gambling. And I'm not convinced he can change his ways, and I don't want my son brought up that way."

I rose to my feet and hugged her. "Always trust your instincts."

"That's what I'm doing. It is difficult, though. I know Robbie's grandparents will be a part of his life, and I'm okay with that, but I don't want him around his father without supervision."

"You have a few years before you have to worry about that." I pulled back and peered into her eyes. "Do you need the day off?"

"Heavens no. At least work keeps me busy. In fact, you and Shar can take off early if you want, once the grooming appointments are done."

"Thanks. We might do that." I could really use a good night's sleep.

We left a little after three and headed for Oakland. Margaret Jenkins lived at the top of the hill in a sprawling plantation-style house. Either her family had money or Jenkins made plenty before his arrest. I knew the man was wealthy, but this was blue blood, old money-style.

"Nice." Shar leaned forward to peer out the front windshield better. "Hope she lets us inside. I'd like to see the house."

"Here's hoping." I parked in the circular drive and retrieved Sheba from the backseat. Although I spent a lot of time in Brad's penthouse, it couldn't compete with this place. I much preferred old Southern charm to modern.

We approached the front door, and I lifted the heavy brass door knocker.

A woman in black answered the door. "May I help you?"

"We're here to speak with Mrs. Margaret Jenkins, please."

"Regarding?"

"Harold Jenkins. I'm Trinity Ashford, the one who helped lock him away."

"Let them in, Ann," a voice called from a room to our right.

"They have a large dog, ma'am."

"Even better."

I tossed Shar a grin and followed Ann to a lovely room decorated in muted blues and greens. A large bay window overlooked a rose garden. A woman in gray slacks and a white sweater, topped off with pearls, sat in a chair by the window.

"Tea, please, Ann." Mrs. Jenkins motioned for us to sit. "Let me pet the dog while you tell me why you're really here." Sharp blue eyes focused on me.

"Go, Sheba." She didn't need to be told twice. Tail wagging, she sat at Margaret's side.

"She's gorgeous. I always used to have a dog at my side, but my poor Lilly died a few months past."

"What kind of dog was she?" I asked.

"A Dachshund."

"We happen to have some Dachshund puppies for sale in my store in Waterfall."

Mrs. Jenkins' face lit up. "Really? I may have to take a look."

I pulled up the website on my phone and handed it to her. "Here they are."

"Oh, my goodness. I'll take two. A boy and a girl. The two best of the bunch. Ann will take care of payment for me."

"Thank you. We'll have them delivered tomorrow." I sent Heather a quick text.

"Now, what do you want to know?"

"Do you have a son named Lance?"

Her expression hardened. "Unfortunately. He's as worthless as his father. What has he done now?"

"We think he may be involved in a murder."

Mrs. Jenkins' brows rose. "That's a new one. Usually, he sticks to stealing cars and dealing drugs."

"Do you know where he is?"

She shook her head. "Haven't seen him in at least six months. Wasn't even sure he was in the area, truth be told."

"Any idea where he might be holed up?" Give me something, please.

Mrs. Jenkins' mouth twisted as she thought, but she didn't speak until Ann brought in a pitcher of iced tea and finger sandwiches. "Please, help yourself." She got up and moved to a bookcase that lined one wall. When Mrs. Jenkins sat back down, she held a notebook in her hand. "My family owns several properties. Some are rentals, some vacant. If he's around, he's most likely in one of the vacant places." She scribbled some addresses in the notebook, then ripped the page out. "I must warn you that my son can be quite dangerous if cornered."

No doubt. I'd already witnessed his ugliness. "Have you heard of Orlando Jones out of Blytheville?"

"The man owns more property than I do."

I mentioned the storage unit we found.

The gray-haired woman clasped her hands in her lap. "Those items are priceless to me. Howard took them when I threatened him with divorce. I didn't follow through, seeing no reason to since he's in prison for a very long time."

"You weren't aware of the money?" I placed a hand on Sheba's head who had returned to my side and slipped her a sandwich.

"No, but I'm sure it was acquired through nefarious means." She smiled. "Are you sure you aren't with the police?"

"We do work together on occasion." I returned her smile. "Why wouldn't you talk to them?"

"I'm a lonely woman, Miss Ashford. Having that handsome detective darken my doorstep every few days was something I looked forward to."

I glance at Shar who glowered. I chuckled. It wouldn't hurt my friend to be taken down a notch or two. It might actually force her to ask the detective out to dinner rather than wait on him to ask her, which might never happen.

Standing, I thanked Mrs. Jenkins for her time and folded the sheet of paper she'd given me. I slipped it into my pocket. "If you do hear from your son, please don't let him know you've spoken to us."

"I wouldn't dream of it, dear. Unless he comes to my home, I won't lay eyes on him. Be careful. He's as mean as his father. It would relieve a lot of my stress to know he's behind bars. I dread the possibility of him coming here."

"If you ever feel in danger, please contact Detective McIlroy." I motioned for Shar to follow me from the house. Outside, I said, "We have a lot of leads to follow, but none really seem to lead anywhere."

"Eventually, something will click into place." She glanced over her shoulder. "Do you think old money interests McIlroy?"

"No, he doesn't seem the type to go after a woman just because of her money." I put Sheba in the backseat. "I hope these puzzle pieces click into place before I come face-to-face with Sarah's killer. I don't want the next body my dog digs up to be mine."

Chapter Eighteen

Even after staying up late talking to Brad, I woke refreshed. So much so, I didn't frown at seeing McIlroy waiting on the sidewalk for me again. "Good morning." I unhooked Sheba's leash and unlocked the door before carrying the cat carriers inside.

"What did you find out?" He asked, following.

"About what?"

"I know you went to see Mrs. Jenkins last night."

I faced him and narrowed my eyes. "How would you know…are you tracking me?"

"Since I can't trust you not to get in trouble, yes. I check the tracker several times an evening."

"Isn't there a law against that?"

He didn't even look ashamed. "I could say I'm keeping track of a suspect."

I growled low and deep in my throat, causing all three of my pets to look up. "That's an invasion of privacy." I dug out the addresses I'd already copied down and handed them to him. "These are possible places Lance might be hiding. Instead of spying on me, you ought to be grateful I can get information out of people you can't."

"Why do you think I haven't arrested you for meddling yet?" He flashed a rare grin, gave a salute to Shar when she arrived, and marched to his car.

"Why is he so happy?" Shar's gaze followed him.

"He's been tracking me. Knew exactly where we were last night. Waited on the sidewalk for me to arrive this morning so I could turn over whatever we discovered."

"Smart if you ask me. Have someone else do the footwork. Do you want me to deliver the puppies to Mrs. Jenkins?" She motioned to the two with ribbons around their necks. "I'm free until eleven."

"That would be wonderful." I headed to the boarding kennels to feed and water our guests. My phone rang as I sprayed the empty kennels. "Hello?" A computerized voice asked if I'd accept a collect call from the women's prison. "Yes."

"Trinity, it's Amber."

"I figured." She was the only woman I knew behind bars. "Is everything okay?"

"Is your friend there? The one whose husband is in prison?"

"No, she's running late."

"You need to contact your detective friend. Something may have happened to her as a warning to her husband to keep his mouth shut. I have to go. I can't let anyone hear me talking about this." Click.

My next call was to Heather. It went straight to voice mail. My next was to McIlroy. I relayed what Amber had told me. "Meet me at Heather's house." I hung up and raced for my car, calling for Sheba to come and telling Shar to mind the store. "I'll explain everything later."

Heart in my throat, I sped toward my friend's house sending up prayers of safety for her and little Robbie. I'd barely turned off the ignition before racing for her door. I'd just turned the handle when McIlroy arrived.

"I'll go first." With his hand on the gun at his hip, he slowly opened the door. "Mrs. Langley? It's Detective McIlroy."

When no answer came, I called out. "Heather, it's me." I clutched the back of McIlroy's shirt. This was not good.

"Check the house for anything out of place."

Nodding, I made a beeline for Heather's room, leaving Sheba to sniff around at will. The unmade bed mocked me. Her purse sat on her nightstand. The clothes she'd laid out for the day hung on a hook on the bathroom door.

I raced for Robbie's room. His diaper bag sat packed on the floor beside the door. They were gone. I sagged against the wall.

"I'll make sure Bobby Langley remains in solitary confinement for his protection," McIlroy said behind me. "I've already got squad cars headed to the addresses you provided. We'll find her."

"Whoever took her won't be stupid enough to keep her somewhere known." If she was still alive. Please, God, let her be alive.

"Don't give up hope." McIlroy took me by the arm and led me outside. "Could she be in hiding?"

"No. She wouldn't have left the diaper bag or her purse." I stood in the driveway searching for a clue that might give me the hope I'd been told not to give up. I peeked in the garage window. "Her car is gone."

"I'll put out an APB. Go back to work, Miss Ashford. I'll keep you posted on every step we make."

"I'll be doing some searching of my own."

He sighed. "You might be the next to disappear. This is a good time for you to close the store and take a vacation."

"Heather is the one who covers for me when I take time off." I glared. "There are animals that need to be fed and watered. I can't just leave them. I've told you that before. Come, Sheba."

Frowning, I went in search of her. Lately, she responded immediately to a command. This time, she kept her attention glued to the storm cellar door. "What did you find?"

I pulled the door opened. A child's cry immediately greeted me. "McIlroy!" I thundered down the stairs and scooped Robbie into my arms. "Where's your mama, sweetie?"

"She must have had time to hide him in here before being taken," McIlroy said. "Is there anyone who can watch the child?"

"His grandparents." I carried him into the house, stuffed as many clothes and diapers into his bag as I could, and filled a sippy cup with milk before carrying the child to my car. "I don't have a car seat."

"There's one in my trunk. I had to take a child to protective services yesterday." McIlroy retrieved it and installed it in my back seat.

My friend had to have suspected danger in order to hide her son. How long had the poor boy been in the cellar? Whoever took Heather had to know about Robbie. Maybe they hadn't cared to take both of them. A toddler would be a handful under such circumstances. These thoughts and more whirled around my brain as I drove back to Tail Waggin'.

"Where's Heather?" Shar asked, eyeing Robbie.

"It appears she's been kidnapped. I need to call her in-laws to come and get Robbie. Will you watch him for a minute?"

"Absolutely." She picked him up and set him in the playpen with the puppies. "I'll make the puppy delivery as quick as possible, then we'll make plans to find Heather the second I return."

Putting him in the playpen wasn't what I'd had in mind, but he seemed happy enough playing with the puppies. I searched Heather's employee file for the number to her husband's parents and placed the call.

"Missing?" Mrs. Langley gasped. "Is my grandson all right?"

"He's fine. I have him here at the store."

"My husband and I can be there in two hours."

I thanked her and hung up, then watched Robbie play. What would I do with a small child for two hours? I had nothing to feed him. The cup of milk wouldn't last long. I scrounged in my desk drawers, finally finding some peanut butter-filled crackers. I bit into one to make sure they weren't old, then moved the puppies to their cages and handed Robbie the crackers. "That ought to hold you over until Grandma and Grandpa get here."

"Mommy?"

"Later, sweetie." Oh, Lord, what would they tell him about his mommy?

I booted up my laptop and did an aerial view of all the addresses Mrs. Jenkins had given me. I seriously doubted Heather would be held in one, but maybe there was someplace not too far from one of those sites that a kidnapper would take his victim.

Coming up empty, I drummed my fingers on the desk. Waterfall wasn't that big, population-wise at just under thirty-thousand, but it was spread out. There were also a lot of vacant houses, barns, stores, and warehouses. It would take a month of Sundays to search them all. Heather might not have that long.

A few customers came and browsed, some making jokes about me now selling babies. It helped pass the time until Shar arrived and kept my mind occupied.

Shar handed me a coffee. "I know it's not morning, but I can see you really need one."

"I do, thank you." I carried the drink to the round table by the window. "I have no idea where Heather might be."

"We need to talk to her husband. He has to have an idea who might have taken her."

"Roberts."

Shar scrunched her forehead. "You think she might be stashed away at the dealership?"

"It doesn't hurt to look. Bobby worked there, as did Michael. Now, Michael is dead, and Heather taken as a warning to her husband. At least that's what Amber told me."

"It's either Roberts or Jones responsible for her disappearance. I feel it in my bones. Do you have any idea who we could contact to get Bobby to call us?"

"Other than McIlroy, no. I doubt he'll tell us. He keeps telling me to lay low."

She chuckled. "You'd think he would know better by now."

We glanced up as the bell over the door jingled. I leaped to my feet and raced into Brad's arms. "You're back early."

"McIlroy called me and told me about Heather." He pulled me close, nestling my head against his chest.

I felt safer than I had since he'd left. "I'm so glad you came."

"Wouldn't think otherwise." He ran his hands down my arms. "What's the plan?"

"We don't really have one. We're trying to think about where she might have been taken. We're pretty sure Roberts or Jones knows something. And, we'd like to speak to Bobby but don't have a clue how to get in to see him."

"Let me take care of that. Money talks. I rarely use my wealth to grease palms, but I will this time. I'll head out there right now and be back before the store closes." He cupped my face and kissed me, ruffled Robbie's hair, and left.

"Don't you just love when a man takes charge."

Shar grinned. "We'll know something by five o'clock. Mark my words."

I really hoped so. I fetched a rag from the grooming area as Shar's first appointment arrived, then cleaned up Robbie before returning the puppies to the pen with him. Nothing occupied a toddler better than baby animals or cartoons. "Sure wish you could string together a full sentence, buddy. Then you could fill us in on what happened back at your house."

He giggled as one of the puppies licked his face. At least he was enjoying himself.

"My poor baby." A woman with frosted hair barged into the store and scooped up Robbie. Sharkbait and Trashcan leaped from the counter and dashed to the back of the shop at the woman's shrill voice.

"May I see some identification?" I arched a brow. No way was I taking any chances of a stranger taking the boy.

"Joe, show her your driver's license. I'm not letting go of my grandson." She covered his face with kisses, leaving mauve-colored lip prints on his cheeks and forehead.

Joe Langley showed me his license. "Thank you for fetching our grandson."

"His mother was quick-thinking when she hid him." I smiled at Heather's son. "He didn't mind spending some time with me. Robbie loves the dogs and cats. Let me give him a hug." I held out my arms, not knowing when I'd see him again.

His little arms snaked around my neck, and he nestled his head on my shoulder. "Mommy."

"No, I'm not your mommy. Do you know where she is?" I muttered.

He peered into my face. "Mountain." He pointed to the mountain rising in the distance. "Man said climb mountain."

"Good boy." I handed him to his grandmother and reached for the phone to call McIlroy.

Chapter Nineteen

I found it hard to concentrate the rest of the day while I waited for news from Brad and McIlroy. Somebody had to find out something about where Heather had been taken. They had to.

The phone on my desk rang shortly before closing time. I snatched the receiver. "Tail Waggin'." I completely forgot to greet the other person with a friendly good afternoon.

"This is Detective McIlroy. We have a chopper circling the mountain and have nothing."

"But Robbie said—"

"The child must be confused."

"You really don't think children or animals are capable of much, do you?" I slammed down the phone. I'd have to find my friend myself.

"I know you have a good nose, Sheba," I said, "but I'm kind of wishing you were a bloodhound right about now." Of course, that might not be much good without a physical trail to follow…a starting point. I was pretty sure Heather had been taken away in her car.

Five o'clock came around with no word from Brad. "Shar, wanna go with me to check Heather's house?"

"Sure. What are we looking for?"

"If she had time to hide her child, she might have left a message only I would understand." I clipped a leash on Sheba and made sure the cats were fed and watered. "Sorry guys, but you'll have to spend the night in the store tonight." They'd be fine.

"I'll follow you so I can head home afterward," Shar said on the way to her car. "I've got to stop at the grocery store. Old Mother Hubbard's cupboards are very bare indeed."

"Ever thought of delivery? That's what Brad does." A service I enjoyed since I disliked grocery shopping. I opened the car door for Sheba to jump in the front passenger seat. "See you there." Inside the car, I sent Brad a quick text telling him where I was going.

As I drove, I thought of every detail of Sarah's murder I might have mentioned to Heather. If she did leave me a clue, it would be something triggered by something I'd said. I stopped at a stop sign and turned right. My friend was clever. I'd have to be just as much so.

I parked in the driveway and let Sheba out. Since she'd found Robbie off her leash, I let her roam free. A person never knew what my dog would dig up. Disregarding the crime scene tape fluttering in the late afternoon breeze, I reached into a stone frog's mouth near a hydrangea bush and removed a key. Seconds later, I stood inside a house that was rarely quiet but was now as silent as death.

Come on, Heather. Speak to me.

I stood in the living room and slowly ran my gaze over every single item. Despite having a toddler, Heather was a very good housekeeper. Nothing was out of place.

"Where do you want me to look?" Shar asked, joining me in the house.

"The bathroom. Look anywhere you wouldn't ordinarily think to look."

"Got it." She disappeared down the hall.

Since I knew Heather a lot longer than Shar had, I didn't think Shar would find anything. It would be something that jumped out at me, if there was anything to find.

After looking in, under, and around everything in the living room, I moved to the kitchen, cutting a cursory glance at the centerpiece on the dining table. I opened every cabinet, riffled through every drawer, looked in every container in the fridge, and came up empty.

Next stop, the pantry where everything was labeled and next to foods of the same kind. Except one box of corn flakes which stuck out a little from the boxes of pasta. Clever girl. I smiled and reached for the box which felt empty in my hand.

I opened the box and pulled out a single sheet of paper. "Trinity, I know you'll be the only one to think to look here. Especially after finding the Jumpdrive in the empty shampoo bottle. Bobby warned me that Roberts and/or Jones would be coming for me. The two aren't working against each other but together.

"Lance Jenkins drove up. I hid Robbie in the cellar. Please tell me you found him right away. I don't know where Lance will take me, but I trust you and Sheba to find me. Check landholdings for Roberts and Jones. Not Jenkins. Lance is smarter than that, according to Bobby. Got to go. Heather."

"Shar! We have a couple of men to visit."

"Oh, goodie." When she joined me, I handed her the letter. "I'd really like to take these two guys down." She pressed her lips into a straight line.

"Me, too," I said, folding the letter and sliding it into my pocket. "Do you have your Taser?"

"Of course. Why?"

"Because we're going into not one but two lion dens." I checked my phone for a text from Brad. Nothing. Where was he? I pulled up the tracker app. Interstate about halfway between the prison and Waterfall. He wouldn't be home for at least another hour. I sent him another text about our plans. "Ride with me, Shar. I promise to bring you back here to get your car."

Our first stop was Roberts Automotive. Roberts wasn't there. The receptionist said he had a meeting. Despite her shrieking that I couldn't go to his office, I marched that way anyway. No sign of him. I ignored the shocked faces of his other employees and again faced the receptionist. "Tell him Trinity Ashford is looking for him." With a toss of my hair, I left the building.

"You can be a tough cookie when you want to."

Shar grinned.

"When one of my friends is in trouble, you bet."
I slid back in the car.

Next stop Jones's New and Used Cars. A little
nicer of a place than Roberts' and about twice the
size. I parked in front of the building. Why would
Roberts, who seemed to be doing fine as a lone
criminal, team up with a competitor? Maybe Jones
held something over Roberts. Blackmail, maybe. Or
threatened someone the other man cared about as
they were doing to Bobby.

"I have to admit," Shar said, peering through the
front windshield, "this visit makes me nervous."

"Me, too. Let's get it over with." I reached for
the handle on my door.

"Wait a minute. We need a plan. You can't go
in there and start firing off questions."

"Why not?" I frowned. "Fastest way to get
answers is to ask the question."

She scoffed. "So, you're going to waltz in there
and demand they tell you where Heather is?"

"Pretty much."

"Why not ask him?" She pointed to where a
stony-faced Lance stood.

When the man noticed us staring, he took off
running. I shoved open my door and yanked open
Sheba's. "Get 'em!"

She took off like a bullet after the guy. I wasn't
really sure she would and hoped she didn't get too
aggressive. He might be the only one who actually
knew where Heather was.

Shar and I took off after the dog, running in and
out of cars for sale. It occurred to me we might be

running into a trap. My speed slowed a bit, but then increased again as I remembered the reason we were running. To find Heather's location.

"You go ahead." Shar stopped and bent over. "I'm about to die. I'll catch up. Better yet, run him this way. Here." She tossed me her Taser.

I caught it and resumed the chase. Not ever having used one before, I hoped I didn't tase myself.

Up ahead, Lance was trying desperately to scramble over a chain-link fence, a feat made difficult since Sheba had a hold of his pants' leg.

"Don't make me use this." I held up my weapon. "Good girl, Sheba. Sit. Watch him." I pressed the button on the Taser and jumped at the loud noise it made.

Lance's eyes widened. "I've been tased before. Go for it."

"Just tell me where Heather is."

"I don't know what you're talking about."

"I can sic my dog on you again. She was playing nice before."

He eyed Sheba whose gaze never drifted from him. The obedience lessons were definitely worth the money.

Shar, still a bit short of breath, caught up with us. "What did I miss?"

"Nothing so far." I shrugged.

"Talk, you scoundrel." She kicked him in the leg.

"Stop it, you crazy old bat."

"Who are you calling old?" She kicked him again.

Seeing the situation escalating, I regained control. "Look, Lance. Either you tell me what I want to know or I sic both of them on you. I'm not sure anyone on earth could survive them both."

"You're going to get me killed."

"So?" I arched a brow. "You tried to kill me. I consider it a fair exchange."

He paled. "Jones said he was putting her in an abandoned warehouse that he owns. I don't know where it is. I brought her to him, and he took care of the rest."

"Who killed Sarah Turner?"

"I did on Roberts' orders." He narrowed his eyes. "I was coming for you next. You ruined my life by putting my father behind bars. Because of that, I lost my livelihood and had to go looking for other work."

"Poor baby." I fought the strong urge to kick him myself. "Shar, call McIlroy."

"I already did." She wiggled her eyebrows at Lance. "I've had him on speaker since I got here."

Sheba kept her eyes on Lance until McIlroy arrived. I pulled her away, leaving the killing thief in the hands of law enforcement. "Do you know where Jones' warehouse is?" I asked.

"He owns several." McIlroy cuffed Lance. "Leave this to the department, Trinity. It's become too dangerous for you."

"But—"

"I said no." A muscle ticked in his jaw. "I'll arrest you, I promise." He pushed Lance toward his car, leaving me staring after him.

"Sometimes, I want to wring his neck," Shar

said. "Other times, I want to give him a passionate kiss."

I groaned. "Ask him to dinner already. Come on, Sheba."

"I don't chase after the man, Trinity. I lead him gently with subtle hints."

Subtle, my foot. I rolled my eyes. "We need to find out what properties Jones owns and where they are."

"I have that friend at the courthouse, but he'll be gone for the day."

I eyed the building. "I have a quicker idea. Let's go get your groceries, then come back here after this place closes. Jones probably has a list of his holdings in his office."

"I like the way you think." She rubbed her hands together. When I tried to return the Taser, she told me to keep it. "I have another one. You might want to consider a handgun. Especially if we're going to continue helping McIlroy bring down the bad guys."

Wrinkling my nose, I headed for my car. I had a gun but didn't like to carry it. It made my purse heavy. Besides, I didn't think I could actually shoot a person. I was a good shot. My grandfather had taught me when I was twelve, but my little Glock has stayed in its case on my closet shelf for years. Maybe it was time to bring it down and relive the happy memories of when my grandfather had given it to me. "I have one."

"Well, what the heck." Shar put her hands on her hips. "All the danger we've been in, and you don't carry? That's the silliest thing I've ever heard."

I shrugged. "I have a permit, too."

She shook her head. "You are full of surprises. Let's go shopping so we can illegally enter Jones' office and put ourselves in danger of being arrested."

I checked my phone's tracking app again. Brad's car hadn't moved. No more texts. I dialed his number. It went straight to voice mail.

Chapter Twenty

After dropping Shar's groceries off at her home, we headed to my apartment. "Wait in the car." I took the stairs two at a time and headed straight for my closet. If we were going to visit Orlando Jones, it might be a good time to start carrying my gun again. I still didn't think I could shoot anyone, but I wouldn't hesitate to use it for intimidation.

"Good girl," Shar said when I returned, gun in hand. "Let's go. Daylight is a-wasting, and I don't think Jones is the type of man we want to spend time with during the nighttime hours."

"I'm worried about Brad. His car hasn't moved in hours. Mind if we check out that location first?"

"Not at all." Concern flickered across her face. "Do you think they're making the same point with Brad to you that they made with Bobby in taking Heather?"

"The thought has crossed my mind." And it scared me to death.

When we arrived at the location of Brad's last phone signal, I stared in horror at a multiple car pileup on the interstate. I shoved open my car door and stood on my tiptoes to try and see whether Brad was one of those milling around.

In the distance, the flashing lights of emergency vehicles lit up the lowering light. So many cars were packed together the ambulance couldn't get close, and paramedics were coming in with stretchers.

"This will take a long time," Shar said. "Do you see Brad?"

"Yes." He was helping an elderly man to the side of the road.

I laid on the horn, waving when he glanced our way. "He's coming."

Brad jogged to where we were. I met him halfway, throwing my arms around his neck. "I was so worried."

"Sorry, Babe. There's no cell reception. I wanted to call you, but these people took precedence."

I cupped his cheek. "I understand." Smiling, I kissed him. "I'm fine now. I'll see you at home later."

"Don't wait up, sweetheart." He kissed me again, then turned and hurried back to those who needed him more.

Relieved that he was safe, I felt better prepared to face Jones. I couldn't have a clear head if I worried about Brad. Heather was enough to keep my brain whirling.

Night hadn't fully fallen by the time we arrived at Jones' office, but it was darker than I'd wanted. Keeping a firm grip on Sheba's leash, and stuffing my gun in the waistband of my pants, I marched toward the office of one of our local criminals.

Sheba's silence let me know she felt as nervous as I did. Jenkins had been bad, but if what we'd heard about this man was true, he took crooked to a whole new level.

The door to the showroom was unlocked, but no receptionist sat at the desk. I glanced at the clock. Nine p.m. The place must have just closed. Spiders skittered up and down my arms at the thought we wouldn't be surrounded by the safety of several people.

"Just us and him," Shar whispered.

"If that's all, we can handle him. Three against one." My words were braver than I felt.

Our footsteps seemed abnormally loud on the glossy concrete floor. Sheba's nails clicked out a similar rhythm. The hair on the nape of her neck bristled.

We continued through the eerily silent building until I spotted light seeping under a closed door. Squaring my shoulders, I strode forward and knocked.

A burly man with muscles straining his shirt opened the door. He grinned without humor. "The boss has been expecting you. Leave the dog outside."

"She stays with me." I lifted my chin and met his stare.

"Suit yourself." He stood back and allowed us entrance.

Jones' office was surprisingly unintimidating. The man himself, far different. Orlando Jones' bald head shone under the fluorescent lights. His square jaw looked chiseled from stone.

"He has shark eyes," Shar muttered.

I agreed. His eyes seemed soulless. "Where is my friend Heather Langley?" No sense beating around the bush.

"She's still alive, if that's what is troubling you." He folded his hands on the top of his desk. "We can't keep her husband in line if she's dead."

"That's not what I asked you."

He chuckled, the sound like rocks in a tumbler. "I can take you to her if you'd like, but you'd have to stay. Cause me trouble and…well, I don't need to keep you alive in order to convince someone not to cause me trouble."

"Where's Roberts? I expected him to be at your right-hand side." I shoved down the fear threatening to choke me. This time, I really should have let McIlroy handle things.

"Roberts is…indisposed."

I glanced at a wide-eyed Shar. "He's dead?"

"Not yet." The man glanced at his Rolex. "But soon. See, I don't need competition, and I don't need nosy women butting into my affairs."

"So, you killed Sarah Turner."

"No, that was Roberts." He straightened in his chair. "I do enjoy these eleventh-hour type conversations, don' t you? Sarah's camera caught Roberts and Jenkins in a meeting at the groundbreaking ceremony of the theater. I'm surprised you missed that tidbit." He raised his brows and grinned, his teeth the kind of white that only a dentist could give someone. "I guess you aren't as good as the newspapers made you out to be." He shrugged. "Still, you are a burr under my saddle, so to speak."

"But why the newspaper articles?" The hand holding Sheba's leash started to sweat. "Why the classified ads?"

"Those were Lance's brainstorm. He thought if he could keep you running scared, you might back off. As for the articles, I'm assuming you had a fan."

I could see that. With Sarah's constant photo-taking, she might have considered herself somewhat of a sleuth. That alone got her killed. I felt a great amount of relief in knowing I hadn't been responsible, even in a small way, for her death.

"Wouldn't you be able to do more in a large city? Why Waterfall?" If I kept him talking, maybe McIlroy would show up.

"A change of pace. I have fingers in every pie, Miss Ashford. There's no need for me to reside in the hustle and bustle of the large city anymore." He crossed his arms. "I'm tiring of the questions."

"Heather's son said his mommy had been taken to the mountain."

"Another idea of Lance's. He suspected the child might be around somewhere when he abducted his mother. Clever of him to throw the cops off his trail." He motioned his head toward Sheba.

His henchman lunged for the leash.

Sheba yelped and slipped free of my grasp. Before I could react, she galloped down the hall. I had one more line of defense. I reached for my gun.

Shar slammed into the brute who tried taking my dog. They both hit the floor.

I stared into the barrel of Jones' gun. His grin widened. "You are full of surprises. Tell your friend to get up or I shoot her first. I don't enjoy killing women, but I will, and I have. Set the gun and both of your phones carefully on my desk."

I'd never moved slower in my life, expecting to mess up and get a bullet in the chest. "Now what?" I asked after setting the gun down and raising my hands over my head.

"Don here will take you to join your friend. I'll let you know more details later." He stood. "It's late, and I have a date. Don, take care of these two."

The man gripped Shar's arm. "Yes, Boss. Let's go, you two."

We followed Jones out the front. The second the door opened, Sheba streaked past us and across the lot. Jones shook his head and locked the place up. "So much for a fierce protector, Miss Ashford."

I didn't care that she'd run off. I knew my four-legged girl would find me...dead or alive. She was our only hope since our phones now sat, along with my gun, on Jones' desk. I ducked my head to hide a smile. McIlroy would follow the tracker and know exactly the one responsible for our disappearance. What Shar and I needed to do was find a way to escape, then wait for Sheba to find us.

Don zip tied our hands behind our backs, then

shoved us into the back of a black Suburban. Stupid man. Hadn't he seen the videos of people using their shoestrings to get free? I'd worn sneakers just in case this happened, or if we had to run. I eyed Shar's feet. Good. She also wore sneakers.

"Why'd the beast run off?" Shar glowered.

"Self-preservation. Her training will kick in. Don't worry." I hoped. Since I wasn't familiar with Blytheville, I studied our path to wherever bulked-up Don drove us. Once we got free and were able to flee, I needed to know our way to safety.

Our destination was a warehouse, all concrete and roll-up doors. Don opened the back door of the vehicle and ordered us out. Not an easy task with your hands behind your back, and I stumbled, much to his amusement.

"Break a leg and no doctor will be called," he said.

"Thanks for the warning." I glared.

The big metal door in front of us rolled up with a screech that made me cringe. We were ushered into a dark, cavernous space.

"All the way to the back, ladies." Don flicked on a flashlight. "I hope you aren't afraid of the dark."

Tears sprang to my eyes to see Heather huddled in the corner. She struggled to her feet, her hands also tied. "Oh, no."

"Don't worry," I whispered, leaning into an armless hug. "I have a plan. You did say you wanted a little adventure."

The room plunged into an inky blackness after Don left us.

"This isn't exactly what I had in mind. Robbie?"

"Safe with your in-laws." I turned and slid down the wall to a sitting position. "Give me a few minutes and I'll have us free." I turned, twisted, and folded myself until I maneuvered my hands in front of me. I untied, then tied my shoestrings together, leaving the zip ties in between the strings.

"What are you doing?" Shar asked.

"Sawing. I saw a video once."

"I can't believe you're here without Sheba," Heather said. "Where's the detective or Brad?"

"Sheba ran off, but she'll be back. I know it. Brad is helping with a major accident on the interstate. Jones took our phones, so McIlroy won't know where we are. It's up to us to get out of here." My arms started to ache. Since it was so dark, I had no idea if my plan was working. I wouldn't know until the ties snapped apart.

"There has to be something in here to help us," Shar said.

"There isn't," Heather replied. "I've been over every inch. It's one big, empty room. You wouldn't happen to have anything to eat in your pockets, would you? They aren't very generous with the food or water."

While they discussed the fact yoga pants had nowhere to hide a candy bar, I kept sawing away. My wrists burned from the friction of the plastic against skin. I couldn't stop. Not until all hope was gone or my hands were freed.

I froze at the sound of something scraping outside the wall I leaned on. When whatever it was didn't continue, I pressed on. I wanted to be free whenever Don, or Jones, came for us. Shar and I were expendable. Heather's value would diminish over time.

There. The plastic tie snapped. My hands were free.

I fixed my shoelaces. Now to find a way to free the other two. I crawled around the floor until I bumped into one wall, then turned until I hit another. Heather had to have missed something in her search. If I had to, I'd chew through their ties.

Voilà. A nail.

Chapter Twenty-one

Holding hands, the three of us pressed toward the door. I hadn't heard Don lock it and prayed he hadn't. Why lock a warehouse that stood empty for how many months or years?

"Where do we go when we get out?" Heather asked. "I'm not familiar with this town."

"We go anywhere but here or Jones Automotive." I gripped the handle on the bottom of the door. Dang, it was heavy. "Help me."

The door rose easily enough with the three of us lifting. I stepped out and glanced around before waving the other two forward. "We should stay away from town. Maybe head into the woods and follow the interstate. We can be home by morning."

Heather sighed. "I wore flats. You two were smart to wear sneakers."

"You had the foresight to hide your son but not wear the right shoes?" Shar shook her head.

"Well, excuse me for having priorities."

"Come on." I led the way, keeping an eye out for Sheba. I still held onto hope that she'd find us. Since I considered myself challenged in knowing my north, south, east, and west, I wanted to rely on the dog to show us the way.

"Why are we just standing here?" Shar asked. "What if Don comes back?"

"I'm not sure which way leads to Waterfall."

"Follow me." Head high, Shar led us across the crumbling parking lot and into the woods where she continued straight.

"I feel like we're headed in the wrong direction."

"We are. Once we find the interstate, we'll head right, maybe flag down a car."

"Hitchhiking is dangerous," Heather said.

"No more dangerous than getting shot." Shar cut her a glance over her shoulder.

"I've decided to leave the adventuring to you and Trinity."

A twig snapped to my left. "Shh." I hunkered down behind a tree, then smiled at a familiar whine. "Sheba. Here, girl." I wrapped my arms around her neck as she almost knocked me over. "I knew you'd come." Now, we had a warning system if anyone tried sneaking up on us. Thankfully, her leash still trailed behind her. I clutched the end and resumed trudging through the dark woods after Shar.

"I sure wish Jones hadn't taken our phones," Shar said, slapping a low-hanging branch out of her face.

"If he hadn't, we'd be found by now." I ducked

before the branch could hit me in the face.

Heather wasn't as quick. "Ow. You could take my eye out!"

Sheba stopped and stared behind us, refusing to move even when I tugged on her leash.

"Hush, you two. I don't think we're alone. Sheba, come." I pulled her behind a group of bushes where the other two joined us.

I put a hand on Sheba's head as she growled once Don stepped into sight. If not for the gun in his hand, I'd tell her to attack. But, I wasn't risking my baby. If we stayed down, he'd move on.

The man stayed there a few minutes, looking this way and that, not making a sound. I held my breath, praying he wouldn't hear us breathing. After what seemed an eternity, he moved on.

We waited a few more minutes before slowly rising and switching directions. I believed he suspected we'd head for the interstate, which meant we had to find another way.

It didn't take long for Heather to start complaining about blisters.

"Hush or we'll leave you behind," Shar hissed. "Your life is more important than your feet."

If looks could kill, Shar would be a pile of ashes.

"No talking," I whispered. I tripped over a thick stick on the ground, just the right length for a walking stick and handed it to Heather. In fact, it might not hurt for all three of us to have one. It would make a weapon of sorts. At least it would be better than nothing. I searched the ground for one of my own, peering through the darkness lit only by thin streaks of moonlight through the trees overhead. I found another and tapped Shar on the shoulder, held up my stick, and pointed to the one Heather had.

Shar nodded and searched the ground. I loved it when my friends read my mind without a word spoken.

I stepped on a fallen branch. The snap seemed to echo, and I froze. When we caught no sight or sound of Don, we continued.

"I stepped in something." Heather gripped my arm. "Please tell me it isn't something dead and decaying."

I glanced down to see the remains of a rabbit. "It's not. Shh." The last thing we needed was for her to get hysterical. Then I pulled Sheba away from the decaying carcass.

"It smells foul." Heather made a gagging sound. "Dead leaves?"

"Yep." Why hadn't we reached the interstate? Were we lost? My shoulders sagged at the thought of going in circles with a man somewhere close who wanted to kill us.

My stomach growled, loud. I widened my eyes and came to a standstill. Wouldn't it be awful if I gave away our position because I hadn't eaten in hours? Normally, I'd be in a deep sleep by now, not stumbling through the woods trying not to get killed.

Anger rose with every step. When tired and hungry, I wasn't very nice. I actually felt sorry for Don if I came face-to-face with him. Especially since I carried a big stick and had a big dog at my side.

Shar stopped and plopped to the ground. "Tired."

I agreed we needed to take a break but only a short one. "Five minutes." I'd kill for something to eat or drink.

The woods were so silent I swore I could hear my heartbeat, the soft breaths of Sheba, the mutterings of Heather. Well, yes, those I could hear. I tapped her with my stick and put a finger to my lips.

After a short break, we continued, stopping at a creek long enough for Sheba to have a drink and Heather to soothe her blistered feet. At least the creek let me know we weren't going in circles. We crossed over and continued. I started to think we weren't headed toward the interstate—a fact soon confirmed when we stepped onto a dirt road. Well, it had to lead somewhere. Since Sheba didn't seem determined to head one way over the other, we chose a direction and continued, sticking to the shadow of the trees.

Dirt kicked up at my feet. I glanced back to see Don taking aim again. "Back to the trees!"

We dove into the bushes and took off at a run, not bothering with silence this time. Flight seemed the wisest choice.

Our mad dash through the woods brought us to the interstate we'd tried so hard to find. We burst from the trees and stared at the high grassy wall in front of us. This state had to have some of the steepest ditches.

I glanced over my shoulder as Don stepped into

the clearing. I raised my stick over my head like a club.

He laughed. "A few sticks against a bullet? You are delusional."

"Sic him, Sheba," I whispered out of the corner of my mouth, hoping to keep his attention on us women and off my dog.

Sheba bolted for the trees. Just when I thought she'd forgotten all her training, she snuck up behind him and sank her teeth into his thigh.

He went down screaming.

I grabbed the gun from his hand, recognizing it as my grandfather's. He fought to retrieve it. I dropped the weapon in a pile of mowed grass. With a warrior cry, I brought my walking stick across his back.

As if my attack had spurred my friends to action, they both started clubbing him. One mistaken hit to Sheba and she let go, retreating a few feet. Good girl. We could handle this scum.

"I give." Don covered his head with his hands.

"Say uncle." Shar raised her stick again.

"What?" His mouth fell open.

"Say uncle."

"Okay, uncle!"

I retrieved the gun and aimed it at him. "Lead us out of here."

"Just shoot me. Jones will have me killed anyway."

"Go." I narrowed my eyes as a car sped by, laying on its horn. Good. A beaten man held at gunpoint by three women was sure to cause someone to call the cops.

"I'm injured. Your dog drew blood, not to mention you three psychos with your sticks."

"Get up." I waved the gun. "You're going to take us to wherever it is Jones hides out at night, so we can end this." I didn't want the man to send someone else after me. Lance was still a threat. I definitely didn't need another one.

By the mile markers, we'd gone a mile before three squad cars, sirens wailing and lights flashing, surrounded us. McIlroy climbed out of one and marched toward us.

"I'll take it from here, Miss Ashford." He removed the gun from my hand.

"How did you find us?"

He laughed, actually a laugh out-loud rumble-type of laugh. "Someone called in that three women were beating a man with sticks. Another call said three women were making a man walk down the interstate, and one of them had a gun."

I grinned. "All true. Do you have anything to eat or drink in your trunk?"

He motioned for one of the other officers to grab us a granola bar and water while another cuffed Don. "I'll drive you three home."

"I'd rather go to my in-laws," Heather said. "I don't want another minute to go by without my son."

"All right. We're closer to them than we are to Waterfall. Armstrong is…well, there he is."

Brad stopped behind the squad cars. Within seconds, I was in his arms.

"Guess it's just you and me, Cowboy," Shar said, wiggling her eyebrows. "After you drop off

Heather, that is."

The detective had that deer-in-the-headlights look. "Uh, it appears so."

Poor man. I chuckled, leaning into Brad and wolfing down my granola bar before guzzling half the water bottle in one upturn.

"What about Jones and Lance?" I asked. "Apparently you found my phone and car at the dealership?"

McIlroy nodded, handing Shar and me our phones. "Thank goodness for the tracker. We found both Lance and Jones at his house outside Blytheville. They're both going to jail for a very long time. No sign of Roberts."

"I think he's dead." Slowly but surely we were ridding our city of the riffraff. So for now, I was safe.

"Sheba found us," I said. "We were held in a warehouse. Our hands tied with zip ties. I remember a video I watched and got free. While we were in the woods, she found us."

"So, she's good at finding not only dead bodies but those very much alive." Brad's arms tightened around me.

"Thank goodness."

"Good job, ladies." McIlroy opened the back door to his squad car. "It would have taken us a lot longer to catch these guys without the three of you. Mrs. Langley, your husband is fine and being removed from solitary confinement."

"Future ex-husband. I can't deal with his lifestyle." Heather slid in the back.

Shar raced for the front passenger seat.

"Shotgun."

McIlroy's mouth opened and closed like a beached fish. He shrugged. "I'm too tired to argue with her."

Laughing, Brad took my hand and led me to his car. "Can we have a few months without me fearing for your safety?"

"You had a few. I guess I can give you a few more." After all, there was still justice to be served in the world and, amazingly, I had a talent for ferreting out the bad guys and helping the authorities put them away for good. I opened the back door of his car for Sheba. "You got a dog-seat cover."

"Since she's a part of us now, we can't always take your car, and I won't have to worry about the leather seats." Brad placed a tender kiss on my forehead. "I love you, Trinity Ashford. Having you as my girl makes me the happiest man in the world."

And just like that, the exhaustion washed away. "I love you, too, Brad Armstrong." I couldn't wait to see what other adventures awaited us.

Book three, Troublesome Twosome, is available for pre-order.

Website at www.cynthiahickey.com

Multi-published and Amazon and ECPA Best-Selling author Cynthia Hickey has sold close to a million copies of her works since 2013. She has taught a Continuing Education class at the 2015 American Christian Fiction Writers conference, several small ACFW chapters and RWA chapters, and small writer retreats. She and her husband run the small press, Winged Publications, which includes some of the CBA's best well-known authors. She lives in Arizona and Arkansas, becoming a snowbird, with her husband and one dog. She has ten grandchildren who keep her busy and tell everyone they know that "Nana is a writer".

Connect with me on FaceBook
Twitter
Sign up for my newsletter and receive a free short story
www.cynthiahickey.com

Follow me on Amazon
And Bookbub
Enjoy other books by Cynthia Hickey

Tiny House Mysteries
No Small Caper
Caper Goes Missing
Caper Finds a Clue
Caper's Dark Adventure
A Strange Game for Caper
Caper Steals Christmas
Caper Finds a Treasure

A Hollywood Murder
Killer Pose, book 1
Killer Snapshot, book 2
Shoot to Kill, book 3
Kodak Kill Shot, book 4
To Snap a Killer
Hollywood Murder Mysteries

Shady Acres Mysteries
Beware the Orchids, book 1
Path to Nowhere
Poison Foliage
Poinsettia Madness
Deadly Greenhouse Gases
Vine Entrapment

Nosy Neighbor Series
Anything For A Mystery, Book 1
A Killer Plot, Book 2
Skin Care Can Be Murder, Book 3
Death By Baking, Book 4
Jogging Is Bad For Your Health, Book 5
Poison Bubbles, Book 6
A Good Party Can Kill You, Book 7 (Final)
Nosy Neighbor collection

Christmas with Stormi Nelson

The Summer Meadows Series
Fudge-Laced Felonies, Book 1
Candy-Coated Secrets, Book 2
Chocolate-Covered Crime, Book 3
Maui Macadamia Madness, Book 4
All four novels in one collection

The River Valley Mystery Series
Deadly Neighbors, Book 1
Advance Notice, Book 2
The Librarian's Last Chapter, Book 3
All three novels in one collection

Brothers Steele
Sharp as Steele
Carved in Steele
Forged in Steele
Brothers Steele (All three in one)

The Brothers of Copper Pass
Wyatt's Warrant
Dirk's Defense
Stetson's Secret
Houston's Hope
Dallas's Dare
Seth's Sacrifice
Malcolm's Misunderstanding

Fantasy
Fate of the Faes
Shayna
Deema
Kasdeya

Time Travel
The Portal

Wife for Hire – Private Investigators
Saving Sarah
Lesson for Lacey
Mission for Meghan
Long Way for Lainie

Aimed at Amy
Wife for Hire (all five in one)
CLEAN BUT GRITTY Romantic Suspense

Highland Springs

Murder Live
Say Bye to Mommy
To Breathe Again
Highland Springs Murders (all 3 in one)

Colors of Evil Series

Shades of Crimson
Coral Shadows

The Pretty Must Die Series

Ripped in Red, book 1
Pierced in Pink, book 2
Wounded in White, book 3
Worthy, The Complete Story

Lisa Paxton Mystery Series

Eenie Meenie Miny Mo
Jack Be Nimble
Hickory Dickory Dock

Secrets of Misty Hollow

Hearts of Courage
A Heart of Valor
The Game
Suspicious Minds

CYNTHIA HICKEY

After the Storm
Local Betrayal

Overcoming Evil series
Mistaken Assassin
Captured Innocence
Mountain of Fear
Exposure at Sea
A Secret to Die for
Collision Course
Romantic Suspense of 5 books in 1

INSPIRATIONAL

Historical cozy
Hazel's Quest

Historical Romances
Runaway Sue
Taming the Sheriff
Sweet Apple Blossom
A Doctor's Agreement
A Lady Maid's Honor
A Touch of Sugar
Love Over Par
Heart of the Emerald
A Sketch of Gold
Her Lonely Heart

Finding Love the Harvey Girl Way
Cooking With Love
Guiding With Love

Serving With Love
Warring With Love
All 4 in 1

A Wild Horse Pass Novel
They Call Her Mrs. Sheriff, book 1 (A Western
Romance)

Finding Love in Disaster
The Rancher's Dilemma
The Teacher's Rescue
The Soldier's Redemption

Woman of courage Series

A Love For Delicious
Ruth's Redemption
Charity's Gold Rush
Mountain Redemption
Woman of Courage series (all four books)

Short Story Westerns
Desert Rose
Desert Lilly
Desert Belle
Desert Daisy
Flowers of the Desert 4 in 1

Contemporary

Romance in Paradise
Maui Magic
Sunset Kisses
Deep Sea Love
3 in 1

Finding a Way Home
Service of Love
Hillbilly Cinderella
Unraveling Love
I'd Rather Kiss My Horse

Christmas
Dear Jillian
Romancing the Fabulous Cooper Brothers
Handcarved Christmas
The Payback Bride
Curtain Calls and Christmas Wishes
Christmas Gold
A Christmas Stamp
Snowflake Kisses
Merry's Secret Santa
A Christmas Deception

The Red Hat's Club (Contemporary novellas)

Finally
Suddenly
Surprisingly
The Red Hat's Club 3 – in 1

Short Story

One Hour (A short story thriller)
Whisper Sweet Nothings (a Valentine short romance)

Made in the USA
Columbia, SC
26 March 2021

35075119R00108